BRAIN STEALERS

Look for all the books in the

VISITORS

trilogy:

VISITORS

BRAIN STEALERS

BOOK III

Rodman Philbrick and Lynn Harnett

AN
APPLE
PAPERBACK

SCHOLASTIC INC.
New York Toronto London Auckland Sydney

ISBN 0-590-97215-4

12 11 10 9 8 7 6 5 4 3 2 1   7 8 9/9 0 1 2/0

Printed in the U.S.A.
First Scholastic printing, September 1997

To Jane Philbrick

1

You can't escape the brain stealers. They're coming to get you. Hide in the basement. Hide under the bed. It doesn't matter where you hide, because the brain stealers will find you and they will steal . . . your . . . BRAIN!

That's what I was thinking after we managed to narrowly escape the aliens who had crashed their mothership in the dark spooky hills beyond our town.

"We" is me and my twin sister Jessica and our best bud Frasier Wellington. Three twelve-year-old kids against an alien invasion from outer space! No wonder I couldn't stop shivering.

We'd been deep inside the caverns under Harley Hills and rescued Jessie from her alien abductors. We'd seen the bubbling lake of glowing liquid where the ghastly creatures were born. We'd been chased down shadowy tunnels by slimy tentacles that stretched for hundreds of yards. We'd tumbled into crumbling old mine shafts that no one remembered existed anymore.

We'd run and run and run. And we'd barely escaped with our lives. But it wasn't over yet, not by a long shot.

We were standing in my backyard, our faces lifted to the sun as our hearts slowly returned to normal. I could hardly believe how good the sun felt after all our time underground. I wanted to stand there forever.

For a moment the three of us felt totally at peace. It seemed like we had the whole town to ourselves. There wasn't a soul around.

Not a person, not an animal, nothing. For a long while we didn't speak.

Then Jessie sighed. "What are we going to do?" she asked.

"We need a plan," said Frasier. "We have to figure out some way to save our parents and the other folks. The only way to do that is to get rid of the aliens."

My eye caught a movement in the street out front. I jerked to attention, my heart beginning to race again. "Right now there's only one thing we can do," I said urgently.

"What?" asked Frasier.

"Hide!" I said, jumping to my feet. "They're coming back."

Frasier looked toward the street. "I don't see any-thing. Relax, there's nobody here but us." He closed his eyes, enjoying the sun on his face. "Chill out, dude."

He thought talking like that made him cool. Wrong. Good old Frase was a real brain and he knew more big words than the dictionary, but he was your basic cybernerd. Pens in his pocket, thick glasses, and a tendency to fall down when you least expected it. He probably heard "chill out, dude" on some lame old video.

"If we don't find a place to hide, we're likely to be chilled out forever," I reminded him impatiently.

"Nick's right," said Jessie, her eyes darting around anxiously. "Just because we got away doesn't mean we're not in danger."

Frasier made a face. "You guys are such wusses," he said. "The invaders are trapped under Harley Hills. If they weren't, they would have come after us. As long as we stay away, we'll be safe."

It's amazing, really, how a smart guy like Frasier could be so dumb sometimes. Because in all the excitement of making our escape he seemed to be forgetting one fact. One very important fact.

All the adults in Harleyville had been taken over by the invaders. They were all acting more like robots than human beings.

That's right, our parents were alien zombies — and they wanted nothing more than to let us be taken over by aliens, too.

2

My eye caught movement out in front of the house again. Something fast and furtive, darting between the bushes.

"There's something stalking us," I said urgently. "We've got to get out of here fast."

"Where did you see it?" asked Frasier.

I pointed. Frasier peered at the spot, then put two fingers into his mouth and blew a piercing whistle. Something brown and big exploded out of the bushes and launched itself straight at Frasier.

"Frase!" I yelled. "Get down! Get out of the way!"

But he just stood there like a big goofball until the brown blur smashed into him and knocked him to the ground.

"Oh, yuck," yelled Frasier as he struggled to push it off him. It was the Grovers' big dog and he was licking Frasier's face like nothing ever tasted so good.

Watching them I relaxed. They looked so normal, a boy and a dog rolling around on the grass. Although the dog was kind of scruffy, like maybe nobody had been paying attention to him lately.

"Hey, Nick." Jessie's voice was low but her tone instantly raised all the hairs on the back of my neck. "Do you hear that?"

All I could hear was Frasier laughing and the dog panting. From the distracted look in Jessie's tense brown eyes I knew that wasn't what she meant.

"That clomping sound, hear it?" Jessie didn't wait for my answer. "It sounds like some huge giant way off in the distance stomping everything in its path."

And then I did hear it.

CLOMP, TROMP, CLOMP, TROMP!

It didn't sound all that far away to me. And it — whatever IT was — was coming closer.

"Hey guys, what's going on?" Frasier sat up and pushed the dog off, starting to get a worried look on his face. Sensing that playtime was over, the dog went on his way, tail wagging, nose to the ground like everything was just fine.

Frasier stood, bits of grass poking out of his hair and stuck to his clothes.

CLOMP, TROMP, CLOMP, TROMP!

"It's coming from Harley Hills," breathed Jessie fearfully. "Coming for us."

"It can't be the aliens," Frasier said. But not like he thought he was right. Only like he hoped he was. "They slither along on slimy fat tentacles, they don't stomp."

"We'd better get out of here," I said, my eyes darting every which way.

"Yeah, but where?" asked Jessie, her tiny freckles showing up dark against her pale face. "We can't hide in the house. It's the first place they'll look."

"I know!" Frasier announced, sounding excited. "Follow me." He turned on his heel and started running across the backyard, toward his house next door.

Jessie and I looked at each other and went after him, not knowing what else to do. Frasier pushed through the hedge separating our yards. But instead of heading for his house, he turned the other way and ran toward the woods that bordered our backyards.

Jessie slowed. "I don't want to go into the woods. No way!" There was a stubborn, terrified look on her face.

She was right. The animals in the woods had been changed by the aliens. Now they banded together and attacked in mobs. They had already made it very clear they didn't want us in their woods. The thought of facing them again turned my knees to Jell-O.

"Frasier!" I yelled. "Not the woods. It's not safe!"

But Frasier kept going. "Come on," he shouted back. "Hurry up. We haven't got much time."

CLOMP, TROMP, CLOMP, TROMP!

My heart lurched. I grabbed Jessie's arm. She made a whimpering sound but got moving. Whatever giant was behind us was scarier than all the nasty forest creatures put together.

Then Frasier stopped. He was underneath a big old

oak near the edge of his backyard. He started to climb the tree then looked toward us uncertainly and dropped back down again.

My heart fluttered as I realized where he was taking us. I heard Jessie's sharp intake of breath as she realized it, too.

"The old tree house!" I exclaimed happily as we caught up with Frasier. "What a good idea. We haven't used it in so long I forgot about it. Nobody will find us here!"

But Frasier had a queasy look on his face.

"What are you waiting for?" Jessie asked impatiently. "We haven't got all day. In case you haven't noticed, they're getting closer."

Frasier shuddered and looked up into the tree. "Like you said, Nick, we haven't been up here in a long time. Something, ah, something *else* might be living here by now."

I looked up. The old tree house looked pretty dilapidated. The door was hanging by one hinge but I couldn't see inside. What if it was filled with hundreds of bristling squirrels, their eyes that strange angry glowing red? What if they jumped us the second we poked our heads in there?

CLOMP, TROMP, CLOMP, TROMP! CLOMP, TROMP, CLOMP, TROMP!

Panic jolted me. We were nearly out of time. In a flash I jumped into the tree, hugging the trunk.

"Hurry up," urged Jessie, practically pushing me up.

I hesitated for just an instant at the gaping door then crashed on through. No squirrels. Relieved, I turned to give Jessie a hand but she was already in, reaching back to help Frasier. Then all three of us crouched under the low roof, our chests heaving with fright.

"Can you see anything?" Jessie demanded, her voice high and thin.

Closest to the window, I turned and looked out. Even with leaves in the way I could see most of the street in front of our houses. "Nothing," I said. "Don't worry. We're safe here."

Jessie wrinkled her nose but didn't answer. The tree house smelled musty and moldering. There were some kind of animal droppings on the floor and bits of shredded stuff that looked like mouse nests.

Frasier found a stick and was starting to investigate one of the nests by poking at it when Jessie gasped. "Look!" she cried hoarsely.

Frasier dropped the stick. I whipped around. What I saw made me lose my balance. The whole tree house shook when I fell. The floor groaned.

SCREEEEEEEEEK!

3

A nail tore loose and the tree house shuddered. Jessie grabbed a post as one end began to drop. There was a hard jolt.

The tree house was falling! It was going to crash to the ground, taking us with it.

If that didn't finish us, that *thing* in the road would get us for sure!

The tree house shivered. Jessie's fingers were white — she was gripping so hard. Of course it wouldn't do much good to be holding tight on to the tree house when it fell. It was almost funny.

CREEEEAK! GRRRRRRROOOOOOAAAAAAN!

I realized I was pushing on the ceiling like I could hold it up all by myself. The floor dipped another inch.

Then it stopped. Nothing moved. No more boards creaked. We were still in the tree. My eyes flew to the window. The view hadn't changed.

"It's like a giant snake," Jessie moaned.

"A humongous centipede," said Frasier. "All those

9

feet. All moving together like that." He shivered so hard I thought I felt the floor move under me again.

It was like a snake *and* a centipede but it was worse. It was a long snaky line of people, marching in unison back from Harley Hills, their knees rising and their feet falling in perfect step.

CLOMP, TROMP, CLOMP, TROMP!

As they came closer we could make out their faces.

"Oh!" cried Jessie. "Is that — no! Is it? It's Mom and Dad!"

Our parents were in the lead. Their faces were empty, their eyes as blank as polished stones.

"There's my parents, too," cried Frasier.

"And Miss Pringle, our nice school librarian," said Jessie. "She always found me the best books."

"And Mr. Forester, the fire chief," I said. "He gave me a ride on the fire truck two weeks ago." It seemed like a different lifetime, back when Harleyville had been a nice, ordinary town.

"I see the Grovers," said Frasier. "I wonder if their dog will try to wake them up?"

We fell silent. Every adult we knew was out there, marching along in lockstep. It was creepy and weird, knowing they weren't anything like we remembered them. They were aliens now.

"What are they thinking?" I wondered aloud. "Can they think at all? Or are they just robots obeying alien commands?"

"Maybe they think like aliens now," Frasier said. "Or

maybe their real selves are inside, pushed in a corner of their minds, screaming to get out."

"Stop it!" cried Jessie, covering her ears with her hands. "They're our parents, our neighbors, and we have to help them."

Yeah, but how, I wondered glumly, feeling a cold finger trail down my spine as I watched the snaky line wind down the street in perfect formation.

But all of a sudden the line veered sharply in front of Frasier's house. People surged toward the house, then stopped abruptly.

"Uh-oh," said Frasier.

A ripple went through the human centipede. People broke ranks and began milling around one another in confusion. They reminded me of ants when their nest is disturbed.

Except this mob wasn't panicky. And as suddenly as they'd broken apart they re-formed again, still with Mom and Dad in the lead. But they didn't continue up the street.

They turned into Frasier's yard and started lockstepping around the house into the backyard, streaming straight for this tree.

Heading right for us.

"They're coming," said Jessie, her voice quavering. "Somehow they know we're here and nothing can stop them."

"Oh, so what," said Frasier, frowning and pushing his glasses back up his nose. "They never do anything.

11

They just wander around like a bunch of zombies, or lug rocks up to Harley Hill."

"Take another look," I said, my voice sounding far away to my own ears.

"He's right," said Jessie, backing up against the wall. "This time they look hungry."

4

The mob surged toward the tree house. They didn't speak but we could hear teeth gnashing.

Frasier suddenly made a dash for the door. The tree house shook violently. Jessie screamed and grabbed the windowsill, white-faced.

The crowd had nearly reached the tree. Frasier whipped a piece of string out of his pocket, tied one end to the door handle and the other to a nail in the wall.

"Good thinking," I told him sarcastically. "That string is probably stronger than the tree house."

"Yeah," said Frasier. "If anyone tries to get in they'll just pull the whole thing down on top of themselves."

A charged, whispery sound came from below the tree, like the buzz of a thousand killer wasps. The crowd had reached the tree and surrounded it. They were looking up eagerly, longingly, like termites who hadn't had a meal in a century.

"I think they really are hungry," said Jessie in a small voice.

I looked out and saw Miss Pringle drooling. It was weird seeing her hair still in its perfect cap of old-lady curls, her kind face just the same except for her bared teeth and the saliva dripping out of the corners of her mouth.

Beside her was Mr. Rodriguez, the hardware store owner. When he saw us his eyes bugged out and drool gushed down his chin.

Jessie and I jerked back from the window and slumped down on the floor. "How did they know we were here?" Jessie asked.

None of us had an answer. My stomach felt gnarly and sick. Sick at the thought of what might happen to us.

We froze as a voice barked from under the tree. "Jessie! Nick! Frasier Wellington!" It was Dad's voice but it didn't sound anything like him. "Come-down-here-at-once!"

Frasier's eyes were big and round behind his glasses. The three of us huddled together against the far wall away from the door. But the floor of the tree house began to sag dangerously under our weight.

GRRRRROOOOOAAAAANNN —

We scooted away from each other and the tree house settled. Then we just looked at one another, afraid to move a muscle.

"Reveal-yourselves-instantly!" ordered Dad from down below.

The strange, jerky sound of his voice made my guts twist in knots. Frasier hugged his knees and Jessie's face paled even more. She looked like a ghost.

Dad — correction — the thing that *looked* like Dad — didn't call again. Instead we heard feet shuffling furtively. Something scraped against the bark of the tree, like an animal with claws. I wanted to look out but I was too afraid to move.

The tree shuddered; the tree house swayed. Something was coming. All of a sudden the tree house felt like a trap.

A thick gargly noise from just below rose up through the floor. The liquidy noise, like bubbling pus, was like nothing I'd ever heard before. It was not a human sound at all.

An answering gargle came from the ground and then there was more from whatever was in the tree. The sound made me feel like bugs were crawling under my skin.

"I think they're talking alien," I whispered.

"It sounds like two elephants with really bad colds," Frasier said. His hair was standing up all over his head.

"Maybe they're trading recipes," said Jessie. "And we're the main ingredient." She swallowed like she was trying hard not to throw up.

Suddenly a voice right outside the door jolted us.

"All-offspring-must-obey. Last-chance. Descend-from-this-place. Repeat. Descend-at-once."

We didn't move. Dread ran in my veins like ice.

Whispery, gargly noises rose and fell outside like waves of slime.

The tree house door rattled. Frasier's string broke like a piece of wet spaghetti.

Then — *WHAM!*

The door smashed open and we were blinded by a glaring red light.

5

A giant form filled the door opening, black against the bloodred light. My fingers scraped for a hold on the splintery floor as the tree house swayed violently.

CREEAK!

The floor lurched under me. Red light stung my eyes.

GROOOAA —— CRACK!

A board popped off the wall and spun out of sight to the ground. The tree house leaned dangerously. The figure in the doorway paid no attention, its head outlined in the red glow.

"You-will-come-at-once," it said robotically in my father's voice. "It-is-time-to-consume-nutrients."

"Okay," cried Jessie as the tree house rocked. "We're coming!"

She stumbled toward the door. The Dad creature disappeared from view, revealing that the scary bloodred light was only the setting sun.

Jessie cast a desperate look over her shoulder and started down. I crawled after her, the floor swaying and creaking at the slightest movement, like a boat in a storm.

"I'm sure they don't really mean to eat us," said Frasier anxiously as he put one foot over the side of the tree house and looked down.

I wasn't so sure. All the faces below were turned up to track us as we descended. The slithering, alien presence in their eyes was more active than usual. It flicked across their pupils with the eager whipping motion of a snake.

Drool dripped from the corners of their mouths in great gobs and puddled unnoticed on the ground.

Mom wiped her mouth as Jessie reached the ground. She clamped her hand on Jessie's shoulder, then Dad clamped a hand on my shoulder. Frasier's father gripped him with both hands and began marching him away to their house.

"Nutrients," Mom said blissfully. "We-will-consume-nutrients."

An answering murmur went up from the mob of townspeople and they began to melt away in all directions, back to their own homes.

Dad gave me a nudge and he and Mom started marching us home. My feet dragged but they kept moving.

I always wondered why condemned men didn't put up a fuss when they walk those last few yards to the electric chair. Now I knew. They're too scared to do anything else.

6

Mom opened the back door and Dad pushed me and Jessie into the house. The air inside was murky and had an odd smell, like dirty sweat socks. Mom breathed deep, a smile on her stiff face. "Food!" she said.

"Yes!" chimed in Dad. "The-body-needs-sustenance."

The door banged behind us with a sound as final as the slamming of a cell door. Then —

SNICK!

I turned, startled, to see Dad snap a new padlock on the back door and pocket the key. He looked at me in triumph and I shuddered as the slithering thing in his eyes glowed yellow with satisfaction.

Our parents herded us into the dining room and then both of them went back into the kitchen. There was some more of that thick gargly noise. "It sounds like marbles rolling around in a bucket full of slugs," said Jessie, her eyes darting nervously. "We've got to get out of here."

But before I could ask how, there was a new sound

from the kitchen. A sliding sound of metal on metal. It sent shivers of panic up my backbone. "They're sharpening knives," I whispered.

"Big ones," Jessie agreed.

Without needing to say another word, we dashed for the windows. But none of them would open no matter how we strained.

"Forget it," Jessie said in a flat, resigned voice. She pointed and I realized the windows had been nailed shut! "This time they've thought of everything."

"But we can't just give up," I cried. "We can't let them —"

"Here-we-go!" boomed Dad, entering with a big platter of thick slices of bloody roast beef in one hand and a plate of bread in the other. Mom was right behind him, carrying an industrial-size bag of chips and a large, gooey chocolate cake.

Back in the old normal days, about a week and a half ago, Mom was a nutrition nut. The only way we ever had chips was to buy them with our own money.

"Would-you-like-cake-first, or-meat?" Dad asked, sitting.

"Oh-cake-definitely," said Mom, cutting herself a humongous slice. She disappeared back into the kitchen and returned a second later with two big cartons of vanilla ice cream. She scooped about half a carton over her cake. It ran down the sides and onto the tablecloth but she never noticed. She just sat down and began shoveling it in.

Dad piled about a pound of meat between two slices of bread and crammed the whole mess into his mouth.

I thought my stomach was too weirded out for food but I found I could manage a piece of cake and ice cream. Jessie forced down half a sandwich. Both of us were still eating when Mom and Dad sat back in their chairs and belched loudly.

"I-needed-that," said Dad.

"Mmmmm," said Mom.

The platter of meat was empty. The cake was gone and so were both cartons of ice cream.

Mom and Dad got up and carried their dishes back to the kitchen. Jessie shook her head. "I've never seen them eat like that."

"I've never seen anyone eat like that," I said.

"It must be the tremendous amounts of energy they used up working in the hills, clearing away the rock-slide we rigged to bury the aliens," Jessie suggested in a shaky voice.

"Yeah. Or else the aliens are directly feeding off them," I said.

Jessie shot me a look but before she could speak Mom and Dad were back. They stood at the head of the table with identical smiles.

"You-must-go-to-your-sleeping-cubicles-immediately," said Mom.

"You-must-sleep-continuously-for-ten-hours," said Dad.

"Huh?" said Jessie. "But it's only seven-thirty."

21

"Tomorrow-is-a-school-day," said Mom as if this explained everything.

School? The word hit my brain like a splash of cold water in a hot frying pan. "School!?" I burst out. "You must be joking. It's summertime, Mom. School is out!"

"School-is-back," said Dad. The thing in his eyes slithered. "All-offspring-must-attend-school-during-summer-season. There-will-be-no-argument."

7

We were still in a horrified daze when our parents woke us the next morning. There was more cake and ice cream for breakfast. It was hard to eat with Mom and Dad standing behind our chairs watching.

"Now-we-go," announced Dad.

At the same exact moment that Mom opened the front door all the other front doors on our street opened. Except for Frasier, there were no other kids our age on the block, but there were some younger ones.

The Grovers and the Costellos and the Sadlers all herded their kids down the front walk and toward the bus stop. Everyone moved at the same steady zombie-like pace and all the adults wore exactly the same expression, that is, no expression at all.

Even though it was about ninety degrees out, I felt chilled to the bone.

Only the kids looked real. Most of them seemed confused and upset and a few had swollen, red-rimmed eyes from crying. We met up with Frasier and his parents at the bus stop. Everyone arrived at the same instant and a second later the school bus pulled up.

A couple of the little kids whimpered as they got on the bus and Miss Ferris, the bus driver, frowned at them. I shivered as I saw the slithering alien flicker in her eyes.

The three of us sat together in the back. "Why do they want us back in school? Any ideas?" asked Jessie.

"Probably they just want us out of the way so they can finish helping the aliens do whatever they're doing," I said.

"Oh, yeah?" commented Frasier, his shoulders slumped. "What makes you so sure this is about school? How do we know this bus is even taking us to school?"

I blinked and my stomach did a slow roll. "Where else would it be taking us?"

Frasier shrugged. "Maybe this is an easy way of turning us all over to the aliens. We know the aliens wanted Jessie. Maybe they want all the kids."

"But what for?"

"I don't know," Frasier admitted. "But if we're just going to school, why do all the windows have new locks? Isn't that against the safety regulations or something?"

Only then did I notice that every window was equipped with a shiny new lock. Unlike normal locks, however, these couldn't be undone from the inside of the bus.

We were trapped.

8

We needed an escape plan. Since we didn't have one it was a serious relief when the bus pulled up in front of the school. The door snicked open.

"Wow. A greeting committee," said Jessie.

Two lines of teachers faced one another, forming a narrow tunnel leading directly from the school bus to the school entrance. The teachers stood as rigid as prison guards.

We watched the kids ahead of us hurry along this human tunnel into the school, their heads lowered and their shoulders hunched. When it was our turn, we did the same. The lines were as solid as stone walls. There was no chance of escape.

Inside the air was musty and stale. The teachers marched into the school behind the last kids, herding us along the corridor. Suddenly a voice crackled out of the loudspeaker system, so loud it bounced off the walls and gripped us like a fist.

"Go-immediately-to-assigned-classrooms. There-will-be-no-noise-or-talking. Communication-between-off-spring-will-not-be-tolerated. Repeat. Not-tolerated."

The same message boomed out over and over again. It was our principal's voice, Mr. Burgess. But he had never sounded like that. He sounded like he was bellowing into a deep well and we were at the bottom.

Billy, a kid from my last year's class, yelled in my ear over the sound of the loudspeaker, "What assigned class?"

"There's no seventh grade in this school," I yelled back. "So it must be last year's class."

"Sixth grade!?" he shouted. "That's outrageous. I'm not going back to sixth grade. I'm not —"

Billy's voice cut off abruptly as a teacher-guard came up behind him and touched his shoulder. Billy's whole body went rigid and his eyes looked like they were going to pop out of his head.

Another teacher came up and the two of them dragged Billy off, his heels dragging stiffly on the green tile floor.

Kids gaped openmouthed until another teacher flicked her slithering, alien gaze over the crowd. Jaws snapped shut and all of us scurried to our classes as quickly as we could.

The classroom was stifling. All the windows were shut and there was no air-conditioning since we never used the school in summer. I felt I could hardly breathe, the air was so thick and hot.

As we took our seats there was an uncomfortable sensation between my shoulder blades. Something felt wrong. Well, of course, everything was wrong.

I tried to shrug it off. It was hot, we shouldn't even be here. But I couldn't shake the feeling that there was something else, something even wronger than all that.

Then it hit me. The silence. The stillness. The air in this classroom wasn't even stirring. *No one at all was talking.* Not a word. Not a sigh. No one was even moving. Every one of us was frightened into total absolute silence.

We all jumped a little when the door swung open. Mrs. Downey, our teacher, entered.

"Good morning, kids," she greeted us cheerily, walking to her desk with a bounce in her step just the same as always. My heart leaped. I'd always liked Mrs. Downey. She was normally pretty cool, pretty straight, liked to joke around with us kids.

Maybe the aliens hadn't got to her. It was our last hope. I tried to remember if I'd seen her out at Harley Hills with the other adults or marching around town like a zombie. With growing hope, I realized I hadn't.

Had we lucked out? Was our teacher the only adult in Harleyville who hadn't had her brain stolen? Would she help us out of this mess?

I raised my hand to ask, too excited to worry about what I was going to say. Her gaze swung toward me.

That's when I saw the slithering thing flick across her eyes like a whip.

"Believe-it, earthling," she snarled. "Believe-it-and-obey!"

Then she walked briskly back to the door, locked it, *and swallowed the key!*

9

After swallowing the key, Mrs. Downey snapped down all the shades on the windows so we couldn't see out. She gave us a fierce look. "Open-your-books-and-begin-to-read," she ordered.

Kids looked at each other uncertainly. Which book? Read what?

Mrs. Downey sat down at her desk, folded her hands in front of her and — nothing. She stared straight in front of her into space.

After a moment her eyes seemed to blank out, like a light being switched off. It was clear she didn't want to be disturbed by any questions from us.

Jessie shrugged, took last year's social studies book out of her desk, and opened it in front of her. Slowly, other kids did the same.

Mrs. Downey sat as still as a statue. *Her eyes never blinked.* It made my own eyes sting to watch her.

Frasier leaned over. "I've got a theory," he whispered.

"What is it?" Jessie whispered back, glancing fearfully at Mrs. Downey.

"The aliens are broadcasting messages. They're up to something," he said. "And her brain is tuned to their frequency."

Suddenly Mrs. Downey snapped out of her trance. Her eyes blazed. "You-three!" she commanded. "Cease-communication-or-you-will-be-punished."

But Frasier wouldn't shut up. "Excuse me, Mrs. Downey," he said politely, rising from his seat.

Mrs. Downey's eyes blazed wider. The slithering thing looked like a tongue of yellow fire.

"What kind of punishment did you have in mind?" Frasier asked as if he was just curious.

Mrs. Downey's head froze in position. Her eyes blanked out as she slipped back into her trance, as if waiting for instructions. I nudged Frasier, urgently trying to point with my eyes to poor Billy's empty chair.

Then Mrs. Downey blinked. "Disobedient-offspring-will-be-kept-after-school."

I tugged Frasier's shirt but he still wouldn't sit back down. "Detention? For how long?"

Mrs. Downey stared at him but not like she really saw him. "FOREVER!"

10

It was the longest day of my life. The sun beat down on the school and the air got hotter and hotter. But we were afraid to talk, move, or even to squirm in our seats.

Mrs. Downey came out of her trance to pass out candy bars for lunch. That was the high point of the day. No, on second thought, the high point of the day was when the bell rang and Mrs. Downey upchucked the classroom key.

That's right. Early in the day she had swallowed the key. Now she puked it back up, right into her hand.

"Eeew. Gross," said Frasier and Mrs. Downey's head snapped around. Her eyes locked onto his. Frasier's jaws shut with a *CLICK* the whole class could hear.

Mrs. Downey unlocked the door with the slimy key. Other teachers were waiting to help her herd us to the bus.

At last we were out of school. We were free! We could move and talk and jump around. Even Billy joined us on the bus although he wouldn't talk to any-

31

one. We couldn't wait to get home and *do* something, ride our bikes, play ball, anything!

But when we got to the bus stop all the parents were there. They were standing apart from each other, hands at their sides, not talking or looking around or anything.

They looked like store mannequins in a window, only their hair wasn't combed and their clothes were a mess.

Mom and Dad didn't even ask how school was. They just marched us home and right into the dining room.

"Consume-nutrients," they said in unison. "Then-go-to-your-sleeping-cubicles."

"But we've been sitting all day," I cried.

"We need fresh air," Jessie demanded.

Mom and Dad just looked at us. Their faces were like plastic masks. "You-must-obey," they said. "No-play-time. We-have-orders."

Part of me felt like screaming in fury. Jessie's eyes flashed angrily and her fists bunched at her sides. But Mom and Dad stood like stone statues in the doorway. We'd never get past them.

Jessie's shoulders slumped. We sat down at the table. In front of us was our dinner — a mound of miniature marshmallows, a large slice of apple pie, and two carrot sticks. I was actually beginning to wish for normal food.

Once we'd eaten, Mom and Dad escorted us closely up the stairs. On my bedroom door was a big, shiny new lock.

"No," I cried, backing away. "You can't keep me prisoner!"

Dad didn't say a word. He just pushed me inside and slammed the door. I heard the key turn with a final click. There was a faint echo. I realized it was Mom turning the key in Jessie's new lock.

Trapped. We'd been trapped all day in school. Now we were trapped in our own rooms.

It was starting to seem like having my brain taken over by aliens might not be such a bad fate after all.

11

I don't know how much later it was, an hour maybe. My mind was zoned out with boredom and worry. I was staring out my window. Nothing had moved in all that time — I never even saw a bird fly by.

And then suddenly the street was full of people. Zombies.

They were all adults, no children. Nobody spoke or looked at each other as everyone marched along with the jerky motion of puppets. I felt a cold hand seize my heart as I saw my parents join them.

But they weren't headed in their usual direction, toward the mothership buried under the Harley Hills.

They were headed the opposite way. And a lot of them seemed to be carrying tools — shovels and picks and sledgehammers. The aliens were up to something new.

I wished desperately that I could talk this over with Jessie. My sister always came up with good ideas and even if she didn't it was better to be together.

And then I felt something strange, like a nudge in my mind, and I heard Jessie's voice, very faintly, like it was coming from outer space. "*Walkie-talkie, walkie-talkie,*" the voice was saying over and over.

Weird. Why would I think of my sister saying "walkie-talkie"?

I turned toward the window again feeling more alone and helpless than ever, when a thought popped into my mind. A couple years ago Jessie and I got toy Combat Talkers for our birthday. We used to talk between our rooms when we were supposed to be sleeping.

Suddenly I was on my feet, pacing the room. Where had I put the stupid thing? I grabbed a chair to stand on and rummaged through the mess on the top shelf in my closet. No Combat Talker.

I could have left it anywhere — outside, at a friend's house, in the basement. I searched through all my old junk, flinging things every which way. I ran across some neat stuff that I'd forgotten I even owned but none of it was any use to me now.

A weight of despair descended over me as I started running out of places to look. I even pulled everything out from under the bed. Finally there was no place left except my old toy box. I knew it wasn't in there. I hadn't even opened the thing in about a year. But what else did I have to do?

I pulled out old trucks and broken models and fistfuls of toy soldiers and — my Combat Talker!

I snatched it up and clicked it on. Nothing. It was

broken. But wait. Batteries, didn't it take batteries? I flipped it over and opened the back. Yes! It needed batteries.

Feverishly I looked around for a Laser Fighter action figure I knew I'd seen somewhere. I finally found it kicked under the bed. Hoping its batteries were still good, I transferred them to the old walkie-talkie.

The little "on" light lit up. A wave of joy washed over me so great that I jumped up and threw my arms into the air. The Combat Talker almost slipped out of my hands and smashed against the wall.

And then I had a horrible thought. What if Jessie's voice in my mind was just my imagination? I pressed the "talk" button.

"Jess?"

"Took you long enough, dummy," said Jessie. "Now listen up, I've got a plan."

12

It was hard work cutting through Sheetrock with just a pocket jackknife. That was the first part of Jessie's plan — to cut through the back wall of my closet into her closet.

She was trying to help from her side but all she had was a metal nail file, not even a pocketknife, so she wasn't making much progress.

I kept breathing in white dust and sneezing and I was terrified that Mom and Dad would suddenly come home. But the faster I tried to go, the more my knife seemed to slip and snag.

But finally I'd cut a crooked sort of hole. I kicked it out and crawled through, getting Sheetrock dust all over Jessie's clothes. The pull-down ladder to the attic was in her room.

While I was still halfway in the closet she had the ladder down and was motioning me to hurry.

Her eyes were wide and strained and she kept jerking

her head over her shoulder like she expected something to come bursting through the door.

Then we were up the ladder and into the attic. Jessie pulled the trapdoor shut behind us, folding the ladder into place. It was pitch-black. Neither of us had had a flashlight in our rooms. The attic was just the peak of the roof, a crawl space with no light.

Spiderwebs hung down and something scurried near our feet, making my heart thump. We'd often heard critters up here, mice probably, no big hairy deal. But I didn't want one running across my foot in the dark.

"Jessie, you'll have to open the door a crack," I said. "We need light."

I felt her nod. "But if Mom and Dad come, they'll see the trapdoor open and know where we are," she said.

"You stay here," I said. "If you hear them, pull the door shut."

"Okay," she said. "Hurry."

With the tiny crack of light to guide me I crawled as fast as I could toward the vent in the side peak. The light wasn't bright enough to let me see if I was putting my hands in mouse droppings so I tried not to think about it.

Using my knife's screwdriver attachment I got to work on the vent grate. I couldn't see the street so we'd just have to hope that whatever the adults were doing would keep them busy until we got out. I was so nervous my fingers kept fumbling the little screws. It was taking me forever.

But at last the grate came away in my hands. Suddenly the opening looked awfully small. What if we couldn't fit? "Okay, Jess," I called softly. "Let's try it."

Jessie was thinner and smaller than me. She could just barely squeeze through. When I heard her thump down onto the dining room roof below, it was my turn.

I took a deep breath, let every bit of air out, hunched my shoulders close to my body, tucked my arms against my sides and pushed. It was tight but I got my shoulders through.

I paused for a quick breath then pushed again. And stuck. My arms were pinned. I squirmed and pushed but nothing budged. My chest felt squeezed. I was starting to feel panicky.

"Take it easy, Nick." Jessie's voice floated up from below. Light filtered up from the streetlight. "See if you can work one hand out."

"I can't." My voice sounded strangled. "I'm stuck."

"Try. Wiggle it."

Again, I let all my air out, sucked in my gut and pulled. My hand moved. I felt a surge of hope but the sides of the vent were biting painfully into my arms. I wiggled and yanked and strained and wiggled some more. Just as I was about to scream in frustration my hand came free. After that it was easy.

We crossed the dining room roof and skinnied down

an old rose trellis that lucky for us had no roses on it. We were free!

"Which way should we go?" asked Jessie. We hadn't thought any further than getting out.

"Not the road," I said with a little shudder, thinking of the zombies.

"And not the woods," said Jessie with a shudder of her own.

"That leaves backyards then," I said. "Let's just get away from here. We can figure out what to do later."

"Sounds like a good plan to me," said Jessie.

We headed behind the house and then crossed the lawn to Frasier's backyard. "I wish he was with us," sighed Jessie.

"Yeah, me too — *AAAAAHHHH!*"

Out of the shadowed hedge stepped a stiff bulky figure with huge shoulders. The dim streetlight glinted off its head. It was wearing a shiny metal space helmet.

The kind of helmet worn by astronauts.

Or alien space invaders.

13

The menacing figure took an awkward step toward us, raising its stiff arms. Had the aliens posted one of their creatures to grab us if we tried to escape?

Jessie jumped in fright and I skidded on the damp grass, almost falling. The creature flung its arms out and both of us leaped away, getting our feet under us to run for our lives.

"Hey! Guys! Where you going?"

Jessie and I skidded to a stop. "Frasier?" we both asked at once.

"Well, yeah, who did you think it was?" He pulled the helmet off his head and grinned. "I got out okay but I was afraid the aliens might steal my brain. I thought this might help protect me," he said, indicating the helmet.

Now we could see it was only an old dirt bike helmet with a Plexiglas faceplate. I remembered Frasier used to wear it riding his regular bike, pretending he was revving a motorcycle.

The massive shoulders turned out to be a loaded backpack. Not a day pack, a real backpack.

"I guess we ought to be used to you by now," said Jessie, who was still shaking a little.

"That's right," said Frasier. "'Cause I've got a plan."

"Forget it," I said. "We're not going back to Harley Hills. We're not going back into the tunnels and we're not — no way, no how — we're *not* going to fight those slimy aliens. I know we've got to figure out how to save our parents but those aliens are too strong."

Frasier just looked at me calmly. "That wasn't my plan, donut brain. My plan is much simpler — and much, much safer."

"So tell us, already," Jessie said impatiently.

Frasier looked over both shoulders then pulled us into a huddle. We were so close I could smell the toothpaste on his breath. "We camp out," he whispered. "That's my plan."

Jessie pulled away. "Camp out? That's your plan? Pretty lame, Frasier. Obviously we can't go home until we get our parents straightened out but camping isn't going to make the problem go away. This isn't Boy Scouts. This is alien invasion."

Frasier looked mildly injured. "I didn't say where we were going to camp out, did I?"

"Not Harley Hills," I said.

"No, not Harley Hills," Frasier agreed. "The school. We'll camp out behind the school." He looked very pleased with himself. "Nobody will ever think to look for us there. We can keep an eye on the other kids, find out what the aliens have planned, and then stop them."

"How do we do that?" Jessie asked.

Frasier ducked his head, fiddled with his backpack. "I don't know. I haven't got that figured out yet. We can plan that as we go."

"Oh great," I said.

Frasier turned and started into the night. "Coming?"

What else could we do? We couldn't go home. We couldn't go to the Harley Hills. So we followed Frasier into the darkness.

14

At the edge of the woods, Jessie stopped. "I'm not going in there," she said. "I don't want to be nibbled and pecked to pieces by squirrels and birds."

"Our only other option is the road," said Frasier, "where we're likely to run into our alien parents. And we know what happens then."

Jessie chewed her lip uncertainly.

"I have a flashlight," said Frasier. "If any creatures attack us, I'll shine it in their eyes and blind them."

But Frasier's flashlight didn't penetrate the darkness very well. We kept stumbling on each other's heels trying to stay close to the light. Roots in the path kept arching up to trip us and branches whipped out of nowhere to slap our faces.

Every time there was a rustling in the trees, Frasier would stop short and shoot his light up into the branches. But there was never anything there.

"It's just the wind stirring the leaves," said Jessie, sounding like she was trying to convince herself.

But we reached the rise behind the school without seeing any animals at all. No owls or squirrels or birds of any kind. Not even a mosquito or a cricket.

Where were all the creatures? I knew we should just be grateful they weren't attacking us but I couldn't stop wondering if they were watching us from the dark and planning something really horrible.

Frasier unpacked and we set up his tent. "Too bad we can't have a campfire," said Frasier. "But someone might see it."

We flipped to see who got the first watch and I lost. Not that I minded. I knew I wouldn't be able to sleep anyway. The night was so silent it was spooky.

I never realized how noisy it was until all the noise went away. No car engines, no doors banging or people calling, no tree frogs or insects, or dogs barking, no bird noises. It made me feel creepy, like I was the only one in the world.

So it was kind of comforting when first Frasier, then Jessie began to snore. They didn't snore loudly, like adults, but even so, it was company. Only, I felt my eyes getting heavy.

I pinched myself, got up and walked around, but eventually it wasn't any use. I was asleep when I heard the footsteps sneaking up and I couldn't open my mouth to shout a warning.

15

I struggled to yell but no sound would come. I had to get to the tent to wake Jessie and Frasier. I tried to get up but my muscles wouldn't respond. The footsteps were coming closer but I couldn't even crawl.

Then at last I felt my breath returning. The footsteps were running. I opened my mouth to scream, feeling a huge wave of sound building in me.

"*AAAAAAAHHHHHH —!*"

Hands grabbed me from behind, digging into my sides. My scream broke off as I snapped awake. Jessie was shaking me.

"You fell asleep," Jessie said accusingly. "It's morning. We're lucky those icky aliens didn't slime their way into our brains while we were asleep."

"Here you go," said Frasier. "Breakfast." He handed out shrink-wrapped packets.

"What's this?" asked Jessie, tearing hers open.

"MREs," Frasier answered proudly. "Meals Ready to

46

Eat. I got them a while ago at the Army-Navy store. Cool, huh?"

"It's brown," I said, picking at some kind of goo. "What is it?"

Frasier shrugged. "The labels fell off so they were cheap. But they're all certified nutritious."

"Mine's brown too," said Jessie. "Except where it's gray." Experimentally, she touched some to her tongue. "Fried cockroach, definitely. And this here seems a lot like ground night crawler."

"No," I said. "I think it's roadkill. Pressed flat by army tanks, a delicacy, like caviar."

"Sssh," said Frasier, binoculars to his eyes. "A school bus just pulled up," he reported, shoveling some brown glop into his mouth. "Teachers lining up just like yesterday, herding all the kids inside."

"Let me see," I said, putting aside my plastic tray for the ants. But even ants didn't seem interested. Frasier handed me the binoculars and dug into his food.

The last of the kids went inside and the teachers followed, marching in formation. There wasn't anything else to see but I kept looking because I didn't want to watch Frasier eat that stuff.

But after a few minutes — Frasier was smacking his lips and Jessie was making barfing noises — the doors to the school opened again.

I jerked to attention. "There's people coming out," I said. "Wow. They've been in there all night!"

"What!" cried Jessie. "Let me see!"

She grabbed the binoculars out of my hands but the image stayed with me. All the adults we had seen in the street last night, now pouring out of the school, carrying their shovels and picks and stooped with exhaustion.

"They've been digging," said Jessie in an awed voice. "They're covered with dirt."

Frasier dropped his empty tray and snatched the binoculars. "It looks like they've been digging graves," he said after a minute. "Lots and lots of graves."

16

If there was one thing in the world I didn't want to do, it was go into that school. But we had to find out if all our friends and classmates were okay. We had to.

Frasier pulled a baseball bat out of his pack, his favorite, an old wooden Louisville Slugger. "If any of those slimy creepoid aliens tries to grab us again I'm going to splat 'em like a bowl of Jell-O," he said, strapping his pack on confidently. But his voice cracked with fear.

We crept down to the school, keeping close together and staying low to the ground. There wasn't much cover, just grass. But all the window shades were pulled down so we hoped no one would see us.

We crawled the last stretch. I kept expecting an alarm to go off or a mob of teachers to burst out and grab us but nothing happened.

When we reached the school we flattened ourselves against the brick wall and inched close to the nearest window. There was a slight gap between the shade and the edge of the window, just big enough to put an eye to.

Frasier pressed his eye to the window. We all jumped in fright as his glasses clicked loudly against the windowpane. Jessie and I were ready to run but Frasier stopped us. His face was white.

"They've got them already," he said in a hoarse whisper. "The kids are gone."

"What?" I looked for myself. I could only see a corner of the room. It was empty. A chair was knocked over in the aisle as if someone had put up a fight. There was a sweater on the floor and a sneaker under a desk.

We circled the school nervously, trying to see inside, terrified somebody would see us. With all the shades down we could only see bits of rooms. Nobody moved in any of them. Lots of rooms seemed disturbed, as if something had happened in a hurry. We saw packs spilled over and papers and open books on the desks and the floor.

"We'll have to go in," I said when we reached the back door. Dread stole over me as I reached for the doorknob. Locked. I almost felt relieved.

Then Frasier said, "No problemo," and pulled a paper clip out of his pocket.

"What are you going to do with that?" asked Jessie.

"Watch and learn," Frasier said, straightening the paper clip and sticking one end into the lock. "Lockpicking," he said confidently.

I watched him jiggle the paper clip one way, then the

other, then back again and around. Nothing happened. "Patience," he said. "And a light touch. It might be easier if you weren't watching."

Just then the paper clip wire got stuck in the lock. He couldn't even pull it out much less wiggle it. "Well, if you hadn't been staring like that —"

"Me?" I said, outraged. I turned to Jessie. But she wasn't there.

"Jessie?" I felt my stomach shrivel up and disappear. "They got Jessie," I cried in a panic. "While we were fooling with this stupid lock, they grabbed Jessie!"

I started running around the building like a crazy man, hoping I was in time to see where they took her. And I almost ran smack into my twin coming the other way.

Jessie smiled. "I've found a way in," she announced.

I was too relieved to answer. Frasier leaned against the wall catching his breath. "What did you do?" he asked. "Break a window?"

"No," she said. "Not being a genius like some people, I just went around and tried the front door."

We followed her back. After making sure no one was coming we slipped around the building and went into the school. It was deathly quiet. No voices, no footsteps, no papers rustling.

I was sure there was nobody in the building.

Nobody human, that is.

17

It felt like the school was waiting for us.

As we stood huddled in the entrance, the empty, brightly lighted corridor seemed to beckon us inside. It took all my effort not to turn around and beat it out of there as fast as I could. But we couldn't abandon the other kids.

I took a deep breath and started down the hall, Jessie and Frasier right behind me. Our footsteps echoed like drums on the tiled floor even though we were all wearing sneakers.

The door to the school office stood open like always. My heart started to thump. What if the principal, Mr. Burgess, was lurking inside to pounce on us?

I gestured at Frasier and Jessie to wait while I checked it out. No sense all of us getting captured at once. I pressed against the wall and sneaked up close to the office window. Slowly I moved my head to look inside.

CR — ACK!

My feet left the ground as I jumped in panic at the sharp noise, my heart clattering against my ribs.

"Sorry," whispered Frasier. "I stepped on a pen. Somebody must have dropped it."

So much for sneaking quietly. But lucky for us nobody was in the school office. The office was so neat it didn't look like anybody ever worked there. The desks were cleared and the computers were covered. There was a fine layer of dust over everything.

The back of my neck prickled as if somebody was watching. But I could see there was nobody there. Absolutely nobody. We hurried past the office.

Jessie looked behind her nervously as we headed for the nearest classrooms, our footsteps echoing in the silence. The classroom doors were open.

"It looks like they left in a hurry," said Jessie, looking around at tipped-over chairs and books and papers scattered on the floor.

"It looks like they were dragged out of here," said Frasier, hefting his bat, his eyes darting.

The empty blackboards stared at us like blank, mocking eyes.

"Maybe they took the kids to assembly," Jessie said in a small, hopeful voice.

I didn't think so but Jessie was right. We had to check everywhere. The assembly room door was closed. No sound came from inside. Frasier reached past me and flung open the door. Clouds of dust swirled up in the empty dimness, making us sneeze.

"Well, now we know they're not in the school," said Frasier.

"Yes, but we saw them come," said Jessie. "And the only ones who left the school were the townspeople with their shovels."

There was a door at the end of the short hallway next to the assembly room. "I guess we don't have any choice," I said, pointing to the door. My stomach felt like it was filled with lead.

A sign on the door read:

BASEMENT
ACCESS FORBIDDEN. CUSTODIAN ONLY

Slowly, dragging our feet, we started toward the door. I tried to make my mind go blank so I wouldn't have to think about what might be waiting for us. We were just outside the door when something crunched.

The sudden sound startled me but it was only something Jessie stepped on. "What's this?" she asked, stooping to pick it up. "Oh!"

She was holding something out in her palm. It was a little plastic barrette like a first-grader would wear.

Now we knew the kids had come this way. All three of us stared at it for a second, thinking of those terrified little kids being dragged into the basement where tentacled aliens waited for them.

We turned back to the door, totally determined. And

totally scared. I reached out for the doorknob, expecting to find it locked. But the door opened at my touch.

We looked down into blackness. Frasier fumbled for his flashlight. When he switched it on, we started down, our pounding hearts loud in the darkness.

Frasier swung the flashlight around but it didn't penetrate any farther than the bottom of the stairs. We stuck together, taking the steps one at a time. The quiet was so thick I just knew there was something inside it waiting for us.

I strained my ears, trying to hear some sound down below.

Then suddenly the silence shattered with a terrifying noise!

RRRRRROOOOOOOOAAAAAARRRRR!
GGGGGRRRRR!

We grabbed at each other as the beast rushed at us up out of the basement, claws scraping the cement floor.

GGGGGGGGRRRRRRROOOOOAAAAARRRR!

18

The earsplitting noise drowned out the pounding of my heart. We ran for the top of the stairs. I could feel the breath of the monster on my neck.

But as we tumbled up out of the doorway there was a CLICK! The tremendous noise dropped off and settled into a low rumble.

Frasier started to laugh. Jessie and I looked at each other, feeling foolish. "The furnace!" we all cried at once.

"But why would the furnace come on in the summertime?" asked Jessie as we got to our feet.

"Hot water," said Frasier, testing his flashlight to make sure it still worked. "Or maybe the aliens like things really warm."

If that was supposed to be a joke it wasn't very funny. But we started back down the stairs, feeling even more rattled than we had the first time. The furnace shut down before we reached the bottom and the silence seemed to rush back in, wrapping us like a blanket.

I shivered although the air down here was hot, hotter than outside.

Jessie found a light switch on the wall at the bottom of the stairs and clicked it on. The sudden brightness made us blink. Fluorescent lights sprang on all over the basement.

We froze. Would Mr. Burgess or some of the zombified teachers rush out to capture us? We edged back toward the stairs but nothing happened.

"I don't think there's anybody down here," said Frasier. "It's too quiet. No way you could keep all those kids quiet."

I shuddered, remembering Billy being dragged away and Mrs. Downey gulping down the room key. I thought there were probably plenty of ways to keep a whole school full of kids totally quiet.

"Come on," said Jessie. "Let's look around."

We passed through a storeroom and the furnace room and some more rooms full of boxes and supplies. The glaring lights made sharp shadows and we jumped every time a pipe gurgled but we didn't find anything.

"There's no kids down here," said Frasier. "Nobody's been doing any digging. We're wasting our time."

He was right, there was no sign of anyone. But I couldn't shake the feeling that something bad was in the air.

"They have to be somewhere," said Jessie. "And what about that barrette I found?"

Frasier shrugged. "So some little kid dropped it after assembly. It's probably been there since last spring."

Jessie nodded reluctantly. I sighed, feeling defeated. Then suddenly all the hairs on my arms lifted straight up. "Wait!" I cried, dropping to my knees. A shiver passed through me. "Look at this!"

There was a small clod of dirt smeared next to a tall box of paper towels. I spun around, looking for more. "There!"

It was only a little but it was definitely earth. Some-one had carefully swept it up. If I hadn't been staring so intently at the floor I would have missed it.

"Here's more," said Jessie.

We followed the faint trail of earth to the far wall of the basement. Wooden crates filled with school sup-plies were piled high against the wall. Without speak-ing we started pulling aside the crates.

Almost immediately I smelled earth and something else. A strange, cinnamon-spicy smell that made the blood in my veins turn icy.

Frasier gasped. "I smell aliens," he said, his voice cracking shrill.

Then Jessie pulled aside a crate and cried out. We stood looking at what was behind it. A large hole in the wall leading into emptiness.

We pulled more crates away and stared in dread and amazement. A tunnel. The basement wall had been hacked through.

Frasier directed the beam of his flashlight into the tunnel. But the darkness swallowed it instantly.

"I think I see something," said Jessie, darting inside before I could stop her. She disappeared beyond the flashlight beam. Her voice traveled back to us. "We don't have any choice," she said, her voice echoing. "We have to follow this tunnel wherever it goes."

My heart sank even though I already knew she was right.

Frasier's flashlight beam wavered. "Who says?" he challenged defiantly.

Jessie emerged from the tunnel, a smear of dirt on her cheek, her mouth set. "This does," she said, sticking out her hand. She was holding a brand-new pencil box, its top cracked and caked with dirt.

"They dragged the kids through this tunnel," I said bleakly. "Back to Harley Hills. Back to the mothership."

Jessie nodded. "And we've got to save them."

19

Frasier peered into the tunnel. "All right," he said, pushing his glasses up his nose. "But this time we're going in prepared."

He rummaged around in his backpack, coming out with two more flashlights and a compass which he hooked to his belt. He handed me and Jessie a flashlight and hefted his Louisville Slugger. "Let's go."

With three flashlights the tunnel should have seemed less scary. But three lights just seemed to make three times the number of moving shadows. None of the beams penetrated very far. It was like the blackness swallowed them.

Under our feet the tunnel was uneven and we kept stumbling into holes and jamming our toes. The darkness closed in behind us.

"Nick," whispered Jessie. "I can't see the entrance where we came in. Look behind us. It's gone."

I glanced over my shoulder and almost tripped over a rock. It was like looking into a wall of tar. "We must have rounded a bend," I said, my voice sounding hollow and echoey.

"No," said Frasier nervously, shining his flashlight onto his compass. "We're heading straight west. Straight for the Harley Hills. We should still be able to see where we came in."

"*AAAHH!*" yelled Frasier suddenly, slapping the back of his head, his light beam whirling crazily.

At the same moment I felt something tickle the back of my neck. Several somethings. Bugs! Spiders! A few of them slipped under my collar and began crawling down my back. Then more. An avalanche of spiders all down my back!

"Ugh!" I flew into a panic, feeling creepy crawlies all over my skin. My flashlight fell to the ground as I pulled at my shirt and struggled to get the things off me.

All around us there was a sound like rain, pitter-patter, as more of the things fell from the tunnel ceiling. "Run!" I yelled, imagining us buried in a mountain of hungry spiders.

"Wait!" Jessie yelled urgently. "Don't move. Stop!"

I froze in my tracks. Jessie wouldn't shout like that without a good reason. But Frasier bolted off into the darkness, dancing and jerking and slapping at himself.

"Frasier, stop," Jessie yelled again. "You'll make the tunnel cave in. It's not bugs, it's dirt. The ceiling is coming down!"

Frasier skidded to a stop. We both realized Jessie was right. It was dirt raining on us, not bugs. My panic turned to cold terror. We could be buried under tons of rock and dirt.

Very slowly and carefully we tiptoed along the tunnel, afraid even to talk. Dirt sifted down around us and over us like mist. I don't know how long we moved like that, hardly daring to breathe. It seemed like forever. But finally the tunnel seemed to settle.

My heart was slowing to a fast gallop when something soft grabbed my foot, tripping me. As I fell, I tried to shine my light on it. It was brown and nubby and rolled away on stubby arms and legs.

"Oh," cried Jessie, running to grab it.

Before I could scream a warning she had scooped it up. "Look!"

I felt foolish when I saw it was a kid's teddy bear, but Jessie wasn't paying any attention to me. "Now we know for sure they brought the kids through here," she said fiercely.

"Wow, look at this," said Frasier wonderingly. He was shining his light on the tunnel walls. The walls looked drippy and weird, like candy that's melted in the sun.

"This is basalt," said Frasier, who was a real rock hound. "It's extremely hard rock. Something melted right through it to make this tunnel. Some kind of laser beam, probably. Something much more powerful than anything made on earth, that's for sure. I wonder if I could get a piece for my rock collection."

Frasier fished around in his pack again and brought

out a chisel. He went over to the wall and started chipping at it.

"Sssh," Jessie said suddenly. "Do you hear that?"

There was a faint rising and falling sound, like waves at the ocean crashing against the shore. Or like the thick darkness pressing against my ears.

"I think it's voices," said Jessie.

I listened again. She was right. It sounded like a whole crowd of voices jammed together and all speaking, or crying, at the same time.

20

Jessie took off running.

"Jessie, wait," Frasier called after her. "It's probably a trap! Wait!"

But Jessie kept going and in seconds all we could see of her was the small dim beam of her flashlight, bobbing in the blackness.

Frasier and I rushed after her. Our flashlights showed swirled and goopy drips of rock, all hardened to gleaming glassiness. Under our feet the tunnel floor was slick and slippery. We slid more than ran. I felt like my feet were flying out from under me at every step.

Then Jessie cried out and her light disappeared. My heart leaped into my mouth. "Jessie!" I yelled, sweeping my light across the tunnel.

"I'm here." Her voice sounded faint and strange.

"I see her," Frasier called out. "Jessie, are you all right?"

Skidding, I aimed for Frasier's light. Jessie was propped up against the tunnel wall, rubbing her head.

"It's okay," she said as I slid to a stop. "I was going too fast. Did a header into the wall. I think I broke the flashlight."

"You won't be needing it," said Frasier in a trembling voice. "Look."

Up ahead there was a faint glow. It seemed to be getting stronger. That noise we'd heard seemed louder, too, and closer.

"Pssshhhhkkkrrrrbbllllllrrrrmmmm."

"I think it really is the other kids we're hearing," I said. "It sounds like everybody scared and babbling at the same time."

"Not to me," said Frasier. "I think it sounds like thousands of tentacles all rubbing against each other."

Jessie shuddered and stood up. "We've come this far. We have to go see what it is."

Frasier passed around his canteen. "Who knows when we'll get another chance?" he commented as he drank, his eyes wide and scared and determined behind his thick lenses.

We moved ahead more cautiously. As we approached the glow we could see it was coming from around a bend in the tunnel. The cinnamon-spicy smell was growing stronger too.

We gripped hands as we rounded the bend, braced for anything, our hearts ratcheting against our ribs.

But the tunnel loomed empty ahead of us. It was wider and the cold gray glow came from everywhere and nowhere. Puddles of melted and newly hardened rock were heaped along the walls like glassy mud.

"Hairy," said Frasier. "These creepoids don't fool around. It's hard to imagine the laser machine that could do this."

Shadows leaped out from smooth walls where there shouldn't be any shadows. They made weird shapes on the ceiling of the tunnel, swooping down on us as we passed.

A winding, twisting shadow snaked over Jessie. She shivered and rubbed her hands hard on her jeans. A large, blobby shape drifted down on me. It was icy. My skin felt clammy everywhere it touched.

Frasier ducked away as a long soaring shadow loomed out from the wall. "I feel like they're looking at us, reporting on us," he said, shuddering as the shadow passed over him.

"Listen," cried Jessie. "It's the kids! You can hear their voices."

Yes! The noise we'd been hearing now sounded definitely human. We couldn't make out words but we could hear the high-pitched cries of little kids and the louder yells of bigger kids.

Hope and fear surged in me as we tried to go faster over the slippery floor. The tunnel grew even wider and the creepy sense of being watched grew stronger as the voices got louder and more distinct. My shoulders tightened against the feel of a thousand eyes.

"Help! Let us out! Help!"

We could hear the whole crowd of kids yelling, but where were they? We couldn't see them.

Then the tunnel widened into a cavern and the spicy smell was so strong it stung my eyes. The melted walls almost seemed to be moving, like a lava flow.

Frasier ran up to the wall, put his hand on it, then snatched it away like it was hot. The print of his hand stayed on the wall.

"Hey," Frasier yelled, "this cavern is new. The aliens must have just melted it before they brought the kids through. The walls are still warm!"

He touched the wall again, marveling at the feel of melted rock. But I could only think the aliens must be close by if this cavern was just made.

"HELP! HELP US! HELP!"

"They sound like they're right here," said Jessie, puzzled, looking all around. "But I can't see them."

The cold glow pulsed at us. The voices tugged us forward while the spicy smell made our heads swim. Then suddenly we realized the tunnel had ended.

We were standing in front of a wall. It was a little higher than our chests. By standing on tiptoe we could look over. "Oh, man," said Frasier. "Dismal."

Down below us, milling around in a circular area of melted rock, like a high-sided bowl, were all the kids from school.

"How will we ever get them out?" asked Jessie.

I cupped my hands to my mouth to call down to our friends. But before I could yell, I heard a wet, slithering sound behind me and Frasier let out a squawk.

I whirled just in time to see a fat, slimy alien tentacle whip itself around Frasier!

21

The tentacle pulsed with glowing green light. Quick as a snake it wrapped itself around Frasier's ankles, throwing him off balance.

Jessie and I ran at it, hitting it with our flashlights. It lashed out at us but didn't let go of Frasier.

A second tentacle slithered toward us out of the tunnel. I jumped out of its way, slashing with my flashlight. But it ignored me, curling around Frasier.

"YIIIIIIIIEEEEEEE!" yelled Frasier. His glasses were cockeyed and his eyes were bugging out. The baseball bat dangled uselessly from his right hand. He seemed to have forgotten it completely he was so terrified.

"Hit it Frasier!" yelled Jessie, trying to dart in, wielding her flashlight like a club.

The tentacles climbed up Frasier's legs and wound around his chest. They were going to swallow him whole! One of them wrapped around Frasier's arm, pinning it to his side. He was completely enclosed!

The tentacle slid down Frasier's arm. It was going to

grab the bat! I had to stop it! The bat was our best weapon. Hands outstretched I leaped for the bat.

Just then the tentacle slimed over Frasier's hand and the tip encountered the handle of the bat. The tentacle jerked away, like a finger touching a hot stove. It writhed and fell away from Frasier's body, slithering backwards so fast it was a blur.

The bat swayed in Frasier's hand. It touched the second tentacle and the pulsing thing recoiled like it had been stuck with a red-hot needle. But instead of letting go, the tentacle lashed out and grabbed Frasier's arm and shook it.

The bat dropped from Frasier's stiff terrified fingers.

Darting forward I picked up the bat in a flash and slammed it into the fattest part of the tentacle.

SQUUIIISH!

The tentacle dissolved into globs of gooey slime. Its hold on Frasier broke and the injured thing whipped around on the cavern floor, leaving trails of green ooze.

"Watch out, Nick," yelled Jessie. "Get away!"

The tentacle perked up at Jessie's voice and swiveled toward her, making slapping sounds on the floor. I hefted the bat and ran forward, swinging at the slithering tentacle.

The instant the bat made contact, the tentacle leaped into the air, coiling back on itself. I ran forward, swinging again and the tentacle recoiled, making a high-pitched hissing sound.

"SSSSSSHHHHIIIIIIEEEE!"

It snapped back toward the tunnel, retreating into the shadows. But more tentacles were emerging from somewhere in the black of the tunnel, whipping their tips around in agitation. They darted at me, glowing and pulsing menacingly.

My stomach heaved and my heart thumped as crowds of them poured across the floor. I forced myself to run at them, flailing away with the bat.

Hissing and spitting, they flinched away from me, writhing and tumbling over one another in their haste to get away. Finally there were none left.

Panting, my heart racing with adrenaline, I went back to Jessie and Frasier. "Well, that proves something," I said, handing the bat back to Frasier and dusting off my hands.

"What?" asked Jessie distractedly, her eyes searching the corners nervously.

"Those scummy aliens don't play baseball!" I said, still pleased with myself.

"Uh-oh," said Jessie. She was staring over my shoulder. Her eyes had a haunted look.

I turned. Part of the melted-rock wall was sliding down fast, like a mudslide. The molten rock began to glow as it moved to cover the opening to the tunnel.

We darted forward as if we thought we could push back flowing rock with our hands. The flow rushed forward, filling the tunnel until the opening was nearly closed.

"We're trapped!" cried Frasier.

From the shadows, in the darkest part of the cavern surrounding us, the tentacled aliens suddenly began SHRIEKING!

"REEEE-REEEEE-REEEEEE-REEEEEEEEEEEEEEE!"

22

Tiny splits began appearing in the cavern walls and glowing green tentacles began wriggling down out of them, like muscular worms.

"Look!" cried Jessie, pointing behind me.

I jumped around to see swarms of tentacles erupting from the shadows and the narrow passage that was our only way out. More cracks were appearing in the walls every second and tentacles wormed out of them in gobs.

They plopped and plunged off the walls then surged toward the three of us, a writhing, wriggling, slimy mass.

We knew from before that if we could make our minds go blank from terror, the alien creatures couldn't find us. It was thoughts they sensed.

Surrounded by them I was almost scared enough already but I knew this time it wouldn't work. We had no place to run to and the aliens knew it. We were trapped.

If we blanked out they'd just wait until we started thinking again and grab us.

We had no choice. We had to fight them.

Frasier screamed a war whoop and waded into the mass of glowing tentacles, swinging his bat in every direction. But the tentacles were lightning fast.

They whipped in front of Frasier, just out of his reach, distracting him while another swarm of them swooped toward me and Jessie.

Jessie beat them off as best she could with her flashlight but there were too many of them. A big fat one whipped around her, pinning her arms.

"Jessie," I yelled, lunging for her. But a squirming mass surged up, blocking my path. The pulsing tentacles swayed in front of me as if choosing the best place to attack.

I could see Jessie struggling, her eyes fierce and furious. But the tentacle was too big. It was starting to drag her off when Frasier broke through.

"Hiiyyyaaaa!" he yelled as he pounced with his bat and beat the tentacle off.

Gobs of broken tentacle flew through the air. But each time a glop landed on another tentacle it was absorbed. Drips of goo on the floor flowed together and re-formed, latching on to the nearest passing tentacle.

Jessie wasn't out of it yet. More tentacles shot across the floor toward her.

"Get behind me," yelled Frasier, swinging his bat like Jose Canseco. His teeth were bared and his glasses were hanging off one ear. Tentacle goo stained his clothes and hung in strings from his hair. "I'll try to keep them off!"

Jessie jumped over a fat, purple tentacle aiming for her ankle and ducked another one circling her head. Frasier grabbed for her arm but missed. The tentacles swarmed over Jessie in triumph, dragging her backward.

I shoved at the wall of tentacles, my heart in my throat, so horrified I hardly felt the slime coating my hands and arms. I trampled on a tentacle and felt it splatter under my foot. But I couldn't get through.

The tentacles pulled Jessie further into the shadows. It was up to Frasier.

"Hold on, Jessie," Frasier yelled, dodging a pair of tentacles waving menacingly near his head, and cracking them good with a blow from his bat. "I'm coming!"

The tentacles backed away hissing, leaving a narrow circle of safety around Frasier.

"Way to go, Frase!" I yelled as he brandished his bat like a sword, clearing a path toward Jessie.

Stamping and kicking, Jessie kept the tentacles from dragging her farther off, although she couldn't get free.

"Grab the bat, Jessie!" shouted Frasier, swinging it toward her while he kicked at a tentacle creeping along the floor. With all her strength, Jessie lunged at the bat and grabbed it. She pulled it toward her and the tentacles holding her sprang away, skittering in panic across the floor.

Frasier grabbed Jessie's arm and swung her behind him. A thrill of excitement went through me. Jessie was safe! We might even get out of here!

Jessie jumped on Frasier's back and both of them swung toward me. Frasier grinned, although his eyes rolled in fear. "I'm coming, Nick," he cried. "I can protect us all!"

But just then a chill ran up my spine. It was a cold, clammy, wiggly chill. But the chill didn't stop at my spine. It began to circle my neck.

I caught a glimpse of Frasier's face. His triumphant gleam was gone. His eyes were bulging with horror.

It was no ordinary chill I felt. It was an evil, slimy tentacle and it had me by the neck. A scream started out of my throat but it was choked off as the tentacle yanked me backward, into the darkness.

B

I felt like I was sinking slowly in cold mud. I kept trying to struggle out but my arms and legs were too heavy to lift.

There was a sound surrounding me. It was a low hum, like the lowest note on a church organ. I knew I'd heard it before somewhere. For some reason, this sound set off alarm bells all through me. I wanted to jump and run but I couldn't move.

The low-pitched sound seemed to grow a skin around it, like thin plastic. It probed at my head, going through the skull like it wasn't there, caressing my brain. It was looking for a way in.

Suddenly I jerked awake. But it was no dream. Or maybe it was but reality was worse. Thick mist swirled around me. I couldn't see anything. But I knew I was alone. Far from my sister and my friend.

That low humming sound was still in the air though it seemed farther away now. I remembered where I'd heard it before: in the Harley Hills, right after the alien ship came.

I reached out in a panic and my hands hit bars. There were bars under me and over my head, too. I was imprisoned in a cage!

The bars were hard and glassy and I couldn't find a lock or a door latch anywhere.

Oh no, I thought, as my stomach lurched.

I was inside the mothership, probably in the same chamber and the same cage as Jessie had been in when Frasier and I had rescued her. That meant there was no way I could get out by myself. The switch to open the cage was on the wall, way out of my reach.

Would Frasier and Jessie find me? Had they been caught, too?

I sank down in the bottom of the cage and tried to send my thoughts out to my twin. It had worked for her. Jessie had been able to call me to her with her thoughts. Maybe I could do the same.

If she was still free. I closed my eyes and concentrated. *Jessie*, I called in my mind. *Jessie, I'm here. In the cage. Jessie, help me!*

But my mind stayed blank. There was no answering thought from my sister. Maybe the aliens had her in another cage in some other mothership chamber.

Then I heard a slurpy, gurgling noise somewhere below the cage. Fear scattered my thoughts like confetti. Gripping the bars of the cage, I peered down into the swirling mist.

A shadowy, lumpy shape seemed to be shifting in the thick mist but I couldn't be sure. My feet tingled with fear. I gripped the bars at the top of the cage and pulled my feet up off the floor, away from that shadowy shape. But I knew I couldn't hold myself in this position for long.

Suddenly a pale pink tentacle whipped up through the mist and slithered between the bars. It tasted the air, looking for me.

A moan of fear escaped my lips. The tentacle raced across the floor and wound up the bars, seeking me. I scrunched my legs higher. But my arms were coming out of their sockets already.

The tentacle wavered in the air. I twisted my legs away from it but the motion only told it where I was. Instantly the tentacle darted forward and wound around my leg.

Panicky, I let go of the bar above me to slap at the tentacle. The struggle was too much for my other hand. My fingers slipped from the ceiling bar and I fell heavily to the bottom of the cage, the tentacle crawling up across my stomach.

My fingers were sticky with gunk and the tentacle kept coming. It crept up around my chest, slipping around my neck and up my cheek, leaving a slimy trail.

Its cold, slippery tip probed at my ear. It was going to steal my brain! I flailed out in terror, pulling and tearing at the thing.

And then I felt something sticky oozing against my leg. I looked and my heart nearly stopped. Pink goo was bubbling up through the bottom of the cage, more and more every second. The cage was filling with it!

The blob grew bigger. I couldn't get away from it! The tentacle eased off my neck and the blob sucked it in. Bubbling and boiling, the blob oozed slowly toward me while I tried to press myself right through the cage bars.

Moaning in panic, I kicked out at it and the blob sucked my feet right in. It swam up over my legs, pinning me. Its clammy touch seeped right down to my skin, making me gag with terror and revulsion.

I punched at it but my hands just sank into its gooey body right up to the elbows. My stomach churning, I jerked my hands back. But they wouldn't come! The blob was sucking them in.

I twisted and struggled to get free but every movement sank me deeper into the goo. It was like fighting quicksand. Only worse, much worse.

The blob kept coming. It bubbled up over my chest and flowed over my neck. I clamped my jaws shut as it seeped over my chin. Clammy as a giant snail it crept over my nose, my eyes. I couldn't hear, I couldn't see.

I was rigid with fear. It heaved itself up over my scalp and engulfed my forehead. I was drowning in goo.

The creature had won. And now it was going to steal my brain.

24

Blind and petrified, I felt something probe hesitantly at my brain. It felt like the cold wet nose of a dog.

With all my heart I wanted to squirm away but I couldn't move. The probe came again, like a nudge. It seemed uncertain. It probably couldn't figure out which part of my brain to slurp up first.

Then suddenly a picture flashed into my head. A spaceship! It was so huge it made the sky look small.

Why was I thinking of something stupid like that? But I wasn't. I — panic exploded in my mind like a bomb, shooting fragments of thought in all directions. Trouble was, not all of the thoughts were mine.

The alien blob was thinking inside my head! My brain tried to yank away but the thing held on like it had pincers.

As my mind struggled in terror the spaceship picture re-formed and grew bigger until I couldn't think of anything else. I wasn't even sure who I was!

The spaceship filled my mind, gliding majestically

through the starlit darkness of outer space. But something about it wasn't right. It looked like a made-up picture. Then the image focused on the back end of the ship where puffs of smoke were coming out. That didn't look right either. A spaceship wouldn't puff smoke that way.

Before I could figure what was weird about it, the smoke stopped completely, the ship wobbled and began to fall out of the sky.

The ship fell straight toward a blue dot, like a blue marble. As the blue dot got bigger I could see it was supposed to be Earth. But it wasn't like the Earth I had seen in space pictures. It looked like a little kid's crayon drawing.

And then the Harley Hills popped up on the blue ball. They were huge, like mountains, and even more menacing and spooky than I had ever seen them.

My panic was simmering and sputtering under the force of the alien pictures in my mind. I wanted to push the alien out but I couldn't.

Maybe it was because of that — because I was so scared myself — that I didn't at first recognize the feeling that went with the pictures. I could tell something bad had happened to the spaceship, that was obvious.

But then I became aware of a sensation surrounding the spaceship. It was a queasy, nagging feeling that seemed to latch on to my fear and magnify it until I felt my brain would shiver to pieces. I tried to control it, to tell myself it was no use to get the screaming heebie-jeebies, but the feeling kept growing.

And finally I realized it wasn't me. It was the alien who was afraid! Terrified, in fact.

At that moment I heard a noise, a rumbling, like distant thunder. It didn't fit with the images in my brain. It was coming from outside of me.

Something was coming. My heart started to pound with double fear — the alien's and my own. It was a horrible feeling. My heart beat against my ribs like it was trying to pry them apart and escape.

Suddenly the spaceship in my mind speeded up. It crashed into the Harley Hills and sliced into the rock like it was butter.

And then everything — Earth, hills, ship — exploded, blasting into a trillion sparkly pieces.

My mind went dark and totally blank, like the power had been cut off.

The alien screamed.

25

The cage was shaking. The rumbling noise was so loud it drowned out my thoughts. But at least I was having thoughts. My connection with the alien had been severed.

I heaved a sigh of relief and realized there was something heavy on my chest.

"AAAAAHH!"

It was the blob! It was slimed over my chest and it was quivering like a mound of pink jelly. I shoved at it, but my hands just sunk into its gooey self and it didn't move.

I jerked my hands back and felt grateful when they came loose. At least the alien wasn't sucking me in anymore.

The cage began to shake harder. The rumbling noise reverberated ominously, its vibration making shivery patterns in the mist outside the cage. I clutched the bars as the cage swayed, feeling my stomach clench under the weight of the alien blob.

I peered into the fog, trying to make out what was

coming for me now. But even though the noise got louder every second, I couldn't see a thing.

My mind bounced between fear of what the aliens had in store for me next and revulsion at the blob stuck on my chest. I had to get it off!

I pushed myself up to my knees, plucking my shirt away from my skin. The weight of the blob shifted, and nearly toppled me back to the floor of the cage. The thing was surprisingly heavy.

Holding on to the bars on either side of me, I leaned over and tried to shake it off. It drooped and bits of goo dripped off and fell through the bars. But the blob itself clung to me.

I was starting to feel panicky. My eyes darted between the swirling fog and the alien blob pulsing on my chest. The thundering noise was clattering closer through the murky fog. And I couldn't scrape, shake, or shudder the alien blob off me.

What did it want? Was it changing me somehow? Seeping through my skin into my blood and my bones? I shuddered violently and the blob held tighter.

Or was it just trying to hold me down until whatever was making that noise could get me?

Both possibilities sounded horrible. A surge of terrified energy rushed through me and I staggered to my feet.

As I struggled up, a shape suddenly emerged out of the fog. I stared, unable to move.

It was a thing so strange and weird, I couldn't have imagined it in a thousand years.

26

Staring, I lost my balance and fell back in the cage, the blob on top of me. It seemed to ooze around my sides, grasping me more tightly.

The thing moving slowly across the chamber toward me bobbed weirdly above the floor as if it were flying. But it didn't have wings. It didn't have anything!

It looked exactly like a big wooden crate floating through the fog.

The rumbling noise was coming from inside it. The crate came closer. Suddenly the clattering rumble stopped. The crate was almost up against the bars of the cage.

I scrambled backward, pressing myself as far away as I could. And then I stared at the crate, unable to look away. My stomach crawled up my backbone in desperate fear.

Any second, I knew, hordes of tentacles would erupt from the slats in the crate and swarm through the bars over me. I stopped breathing.

"Nick?"

The crate spoke. It was a hissing, whispery sound. My heart punched against my lungs. They knew my name!

"Nick? Are you okay?"

I felt sick. The aliens even knew how to imitate my sister's voice.

"Nick, it's me!" The crate rumbled closer until it touched the bars. "Can you answer me?"

Through the slats I saw Jessie's eyes peering anxiously into my face. In my excitement I forgot about the thing on my chest and bolted upright, or tried to. "Jessie! How did you find me? What is this thing?" I asked, gesturing at the crate. "Where did it come from?"

"No time for explanations," said Jessie. "We've got to get you out of here." Then I saw her eyes go wide with fear when she saw the glistening horror that covered me from neck to waist. "Oh, no," she whispered. "Are we too late? Did they get you?"

"No," I said uncertainly. "I don't think so."

"What's going on?" said a second voice inside the crate. "Do you see any tentacles?"

"Frasier!" I cried.

"Yeah, man. We're going to save you," promised Frasier's voice, sounding muffled. "You'll be okay in here."

Clattering over the floor the crate began moving away.

What were they doing? Weren't they going to get me out of here? They couldn't just leave me!

The crate stopped beside the wall and Frasier's arm reached out. He was holding the baseball bat. He pushed and jiggled it up along the wall until he managed to hit the switch that opened the cage.

As the side of the cage swung open and the crate moved back toward me, the alien shot out two short tentacles and grabbed the bars of the cage behind me. It was trying to keep me here!

Fury shot through me. I twisted and broke the alien's hold more quickly than I expected to. I lost my balance. I grabbed at the cage to catch myself but the door had swung away.

The crate was still too far off.

I looked down. Fog swirled below me. Down there was the place the blobs bubbled up from. My stomach turned inside out. I was about to fall right into it.

I toppled out of the cage into the murky fog and shut my eyes. All my insides crawled away from my skin.

Then suddenly I bounced in midair. My eyes snapped open. I was suspended half out of the cage and I was bouncing like a ball on a rubber band.

It was the alien. It had shot out a tentacle and held on to the cage. But already its hold was slipping, the tentacle sliding slowly off the bar. I quickly hauled myself back into the cage opening just as the wooden crate pulled up.

The front panel slid open. Jessie's face looked scared,

anxious for me, and sick with loathing at the sight of the pink, pus-colored alien. She reached behind her for Frasier's bat.

"Hold on, Nick," she said. "I'll get rid of that thing for you."

But as she put her hand on the bat, a horrible shriek pierced our ears, freezing us in place.

REEEE-REEEEE-REEEEEE-RREEEE.

Jessie's eyes filled with terror as she looked behind me. I glanced back.

A mass of screaming tentacles was whipping toward me from out of the fog behind the cage.

REEEEEEEEEE-REEEEEEEEEE-REEEEEEEEEEEEEE!

27

"Quick!" Frasier shouted. "Jump in the crate. You'll be safe in here!"

A tentacle strafed the air over my head. The blob on my chest started to crawl up my neck.

I jumped.

Jessie screamed and fell backward into Frasier. "Whoa, careful," Frasier yelled, pushing her up. "Get behind me so I can steer." Then he caught sight of what was in the crate with us — the blob on my chest.

His eyes bulged and he grabbed the bat.

"Wait!" I shouted as the blob wrapped itself wetly around my neck, trying to crawl over my shoulder. I shuddered with revulsion but held my hand up to keep Frasier's bat from striking the alien.

Outside the crate a storm of tentacles shrieked. One of them whipped inside the opening of the crate and lashed at my head.

I reached behind me and grabbed the sliding wooden

panel of the crate. The tentacle hissed in fury and re-coiled. I slammed the panel shut.

"Come on," I shouted. "Let's get out of here!"

It was dark inside with the door shut. The only light came through the slats in the sides. We could see tenta-cles writhing in frenzy outside. But they didn't smash into the crate.

I heard more than saw Frasier scrambling up. As my eyes adjusted to the dark I saw he had his bike rigged inside the crate to propel it. He climbed onto the seat, trying to keep his knees from knocking into me.

We were pretty squeezed together in there. I couldn't sit up straight and my chin was almost mashed into the alien goo still clinging stickily to my chest.

"I think they got to his brain," Jessie whispered fear-fully to Frasier.

"No, they didn't," I said irritably. Or had they? The thought nagged at the back of my mind like a splinter. "I have a plan." But did I really? Was it my plan? Or the aliens'?

Just then a tentacle whizzed shrieking by the slat near my ear and I flinched.

REEEEE-REEEEEEEEE!

The crate rocked from the turbulence created by the thrashing tentacles.

Frasier adjusted his feet on the bicycle pedals. "Relax," he said. "They can't get to us in here. You know why?"

I thought I did but before I could say it, Frasier said, "Wood! The aliens hate wood! That's why the baseball bat worked."

"You mean like Superman and kryptonite?"

"Something like that, yeah. I think," said Frasier. "All we really know is they'll do almost anything to avoid wood. So we're safe in here." He eyed the thing on my chest. "Except for that."

"But how did you do this?" I asked, mystified. "Where did this contraption come from?"

Frasier grinned, proud of himself. "After the aliens got you, they were so distracted we managed to escape back down the tunnel to the school. I worked it out about the wood while we were running and remembered all those crates we had to move."

Suddenly Jessie spoke up, her voice shaky. "Frasier, I think we better head out of here. They look like they're going to attack."

"They wouldn't dare!" But he sounded uncertain.

But even as Frasier hurried to turn the crate around, he kept talking. "I realized we needed a way to maneuver the crate from inside. My bike was an obvious solution. Luckily all the adults are still off somewhere doing aliens know what, so it was no problem getting the bike. Mounting the crate on it was a serious feat of engineering, however."

"Hurry, Frasier!" urged Jessie.

I peered out the narrow slat. The tentacles were more frantic than ever. They'd coiled into a writhing mass and it seemed like they were getting ready to hurl them-selves at us, all together, no matter how much it hurt.

Frasier pedaled hard and wrenched the handlebars. The crate wobbled. The alien pressed itself against me, its sliminess seeping through my shirt.

Frasier kept talking. "First I had to get the balance just right," he said. "Later you'll see the supports over the front and rear fenders —"

"Save it, Frasier!" yelled Jessie. "Later!"

The crate dipped. I felt myself slip and reached out to grab the sides. But there was nothing to hold on to.

"Stay still," Frasier commanded nervously. "I had to work fast so this thing isn't very stable. We need to keep our weight balanced."

I forced myself not to move even though I felt we were going to topple over. Slowly Frasier maneuvered the awkward vehicle around and got it headed toward the entrance.

REEEEEEEEEEE-REEEEEEEEEEEE-REEEEEEEEEEEEE!

The piercing shrieks grew deafening. Pain ricocheted through my ears. I risked another glance through the slat.

The pulsing tentacles were twisting and untwisting together in a mad riot. It was like they wanted more than anything to attack us but couldn't.

Then suddenly there was a new sound.

HSSSSSSSSHSSSSSSSHS!

A wave of heat struck the crate like a blow and a strange hot smell washed over us.

Outside the crate the agitated fog began to glow. And then I saw it wasn't the mist that was glowing but the chamber wall nearest us.

As we stared, the edges of the wall began to melt. The rock sizzled and bubbled, turning to liquid before our eyes.

"No!" cried Jessie. "They're going to bury us in molten rock!"

28

Frasier pedaled furiously for the entrance as all around us rock smoked and hissed.

Through the slats we could see the wall bubbling. Pockets of gas erupted into flame. Liquefied rock flowed down and slid straight into our path. Frasier veered and the bike tilted dangerously.

The tentacles shrieked gleefully, unharmed by the boiling streams of rock.

Ahead of us the entrance began to melt, stones tumbling and dissolving against one another. Frasier pedaled harder. But the bike moved sluggishly, going slower and slower the harder he worked.

"The tires must be melting!" Frasier shouted over the noise of tumbling, superheated rock.

At that moment a big slab of the wall crashed into our path. A geyser of steam shot into the air. The rock melted like butter in a hot pan, bubbling furiously and spattering glowing drops in all directions.

Jessie cried out and threw her arms over her head.

Frasier labored to turn the bike. We had to find a new path to the entrance, but how? Everywhere we looked puddles of boiling rock melted holes in the chamber floor.

"Look!" cried Jessie in shock.

I turned my head just in time to see the two walls of the entrance come crashing together in a burst of flame. The walls flowed together in a molten river of glowing orange that was strangely beautiful.

Our hopes vanished with a burp of steam. Now there was no way out of here. We stared at the horrible beauty as if mesmerized, watching the rock throw tongues of blue and red flame among the bubbling pools and streams.

Over our heads rock sputtered and exploded, battering the crate with shards of glowing stone.

Any second the wood would burst into flame. If the flames didn't get us, if the molten rock somehow didn't get us, then the aliens would — the instant the wood went up in smoke leaving us unprotected.

But I didn't think we had to worry about lasting that long.

The alien blob on my chest began to bubble too, as if imitating the rock. It formed a small tentacle which snaked up toward my ear.

Jessie and Frasier, too horrified by the sight outside our crate, didn't notice. But I couldn't stand another second of boiling alive with an alien bag of goo slimed to my chest.

I turned and flung open the sliding crate panel. Heat struck my face like a slap.

"Come on," I shrieked. "Come and get me."

REEEEEEE-REEEEEEEEEE-REEEEEEEEEE!

The alien tentacles tumbled over themselves to get to me, their slimy tips dripping with anticipation.

29

Behind me Frasier and Jessie screamed. "Nick! What are you doing?"

Someone grabbed the back of my shirt. The crate rocked dangerously.

"Keep back," I shouted, twisting away.

Hands grabbed again for my shirt. The aliens were close, knocking each other aside to be the first to get me. I reached behind me and shoved at the hands holding me.

"Trust me," I shouted. "And keep back. Don't let the crate fall over."

I shut out their arguing voices. I needed all my concentration.

I waited until the tentacles were so close I could almost touch them. Then I swung myself sideways, so the alien stuck to me was no more than an inch from the wooden edge of the crate.

The blob bubbled and flattened against me, making small squealing noises. The approaching tentacles stopped dead, their tips quivering.

I focused my thoughts at the tentacles although I didn't think they could understand. "Let us out," I demanded loudly. "Let us out this instant or I will mash your friend against this wood. And that's a promise!"

The tentacles recoiled, shrieking and slapping against one another. I went through the whole thing again, using lots of sign language. I pointed at me, at the closed-up glowing former entrance, at the blob sputtering slime all over my shirt.

"Out!" I screamed.

The tentacles backed off. As quickly as it had come the heat went out of the rock walls around us. The steam died down and the flames and colors disappeared. The rock stopped flowing.

Frasier gasped. Before us was a new glow. The entrance was glowing again but this time the glow was burning a hole — a way out!

The hole grew wider. The tentacles were backed against the walls, swaying slightly and silent.

"We're outta here!" whooped Frasier, standing on the pedals. The bike didn't work very well but at least it moved. And we were still safe inside our crate.

We rode out of the chamber and found ourselves in the vast cavern of the mothership, the place I remembered as their control room. But before we could look around and get any ideas, another hole opened on the far side of the control room.

Through it we could see what looked like daylight!

"Oh, yes," breathed Frasier thankfully, and started pedaling with all his might.

Th-wunk, Th-wunk.

The tires were definitely flat. I looked behind us. The chamber entrance was filled with fat, hissing tentacles, pulsing and glowing with purple light.

"Come on, bike," Jessie urged. "Just a little farther. Just a little more."

Th-wunk, Th-wunk, Th-wunk.

The bike limped across the cavern and bumped on into the tunnel. Sunshine slatted across the melted-rock floor.

I looked over my shoulder. The tentacles were slithering across the cavern after us. My heart flip-flopped but when I turned to see how much farther we had to go, we were there! Outside!

Frasier stopped the bike. We were on the slope of Harley Hill, the tallest of the barren rocky hills west of town.

I climbed out of the crate so Frasier and Jessie could get out but I kept my hand on the wood at all times. I wasn't taking any chances with our resident alien.

"We made it," cried Frasier, high-fiving me and Jessie and me again. We were all laughing and ready to collapse with relief.

"I guess you were right bringing that alien," said

Frasier. He reached into the crate and brought out his baseball bat. "But now it's time to get the slimy little sucker off you, don't you think? Its friends can come and collect it when we leave."

My flesh crawled. More than anything I wanted to do what Frasier said — get this revolting thing off me and run from this place as fast as I could. But —

"We might be safe — for now — but the aliens still have our school friends," I said. "Our parents are still taken over by them. The aliens are too strong for us. We'll never save everybody and get rid of them on our own."

Frasier's eyes narrowed. He straightened his glasses and looked back at the new tunnel, its melted rock surface still glistening in the sun. Jessie looked at the little alien as if she had an apple stuck in her throat.

The alien was pulsing rapidly. It looked like a huge beating heart made out of half-melted gummy bears.

"What's your plan?" asked Jessie cautiously.

"Uh-oh," said Frasier. He was looking over my shoulder, down the hill. "All plans on hold for the moment, guys. We got trouble coming."

I turned, careful not to scrape the alien against the wooden crate. Marching up the hill in zombie formation were all of Harleyville's adults.

They were hefting pickaxes and shovels and making straight for us. Their eyes were stone-cold except for the slithering thing that glowed in their depths.

30

"Run!" shouted Frasier.

"Wait!" I demanded. "We need the crate. For the alien."

Frasier bit his lip and threw a worried glance down the hill. The townspeople were getting closer. I could make out Mom and Dad marching in front. Frasier's parents were close behind.

Soon it would be too late to run.

"Come on, Frasier, help me get the crate off the bike," urged Jessie, struggling with it. "Hurry. Nick can't help. Not with that *thing* stuck on him."

Frasier gritted his teeth and helped Jessie wiggle the big crate up off the bicycle.

It was eerie the way the adults kept staring at us without making a sound. They marched steadily, not even speeding up when we got the crate free.

We headed off along the side of the hill, our feet slipping and sliding on the pebbles and loose dirt. Pebbles bounced down the hill. I winced when one of them struck Mr. Burgess, our principal, but he didn't flinch, like he never felt it.

The little alien hanging off me jounced like a big sack of overripe tomatoes. Slime ran down my pant legs and dripped onto my sneakers. My stomach curdled but I kept going.

With Frasier and Jessie carrying the crate between them, and me burdened as I was, we couldn't go very fast. I looked down the hillside and my heart sank like a lead sinker.

The adults were veering off along the hill below, cutting us off.

"We're not going to make it," said Jessie. She looked grimly at me, wiping sweat off her forehead. "If you really have a plan, Nick, now's the time to tell us."

"We hold the alien for ransom," I said between panting breaths. "They give us back the other kids and make our parents normal again and we return their friend."

"We have to make them leave, too," said Jessie, breathing hard and casting worried glances down the hill. "Otherwise what's to stop them from doing it all over again?"

"Mmm," I said thoughtfully. "There could be a problem with that. With them leaving. The alien ship seems to have broken down."

Frasier's head jerked up as he shot me a startled look. "How —?" But the sudden movement made him slip on the steep pebbly surface. He stumbled and let go of the crate. His end hit the ground with a crunch.

The corner of the crate was splintered. Frasier's knee was wrenched and he couldn't run.

The adults closed in, their blank faces showing no change of expression. Our own parents and friends, and they were going to hand us back to the aliens.

And at this point, the aliens were *really* mad.

My dad stepped out of the crowd. His eyes glowed as the alien slither whiplashed furiously inside them.

I shivered so hard a hefty gob of slime dripped onto my hand. My plans were unraveling before my eyes.

Suddenly I felt in my bones that the whole town was doomed.

31

"Earthling-Nicholas," said my dad in his dead, robotic voice. "You-will-leave-what-does-not-belong-to-you-and-join-the-other-children-at-once."

"Yeah, right," whispered Frasier sarcastically. "Tell him our terms, Nick."

"No!" Jessie started to grab my arm then thought better of it, making a face as she rubbed her fingers against her T-shirt. "We can't let the alien go until we figure out how to make them leave our planet."

Frasier nodded. "Tell them we'll deliver the alien as soon as their engines are revved up and our parents and friends are free."

I nodded. "Sorry, Dad," I called out. "But we're keeping this alien captive until all you guys are free and our friends too and the alien spaceship is ready to leave Earth."

But Dad didn't seem to hear a word.

"Earthling, you-must-join-the-other-children," he said.

Mom stepped up beside him. "No-harm-will-come-to-you-if-you-do-as-we-say," she announced flatly.

And then they both started toward us, arms stretched out in front of them like Frankenstein, the thing in their eyes slithering madly back and forth.

Frasier's parents stepped out of the mob and fell in behind Mom and Dad.

Then the other adults threw aside their shovels and picks. They fell into formation too. Their eyes glowed but they weren't seeing us. Not the real us. All they saw were objects that were in their way.

They marched toward us, faces slack, arms reaching out, their hands twitching like eager claws.

"They're going to grab us!" cried Jessie. "They don't care about the little alien!"

I jumped behind the crate. "Stop!" I ordered, pointing at the quivering alien on my chest. "Stop now or I'll make a wood sandwich out of this little slimeball!"

They kept coming.

"Stop!" I shouted hoarsely. If they dragged us down into that cavern, none of us would ever be free or human again. My heart pounded as the alien pulsed wildly against my chest.

They kept coming. I stood tall, my belly inches from the edge of the crate. "I warned you," I yelled. "In five seconds I'm going to mash this alien! One . . ."

It was like they didn't hear me. "Two . . . three . . ."

Suddenly Frasier's parents plunged out of formation and pounced on Frasier, each one grabbing an arm.

"Noooooo," he screamed. "Nick, do it, wood the alien, hurry!"

I felt paralyzed with horror. Gritting my teeth, I leaned closer to the wooden crate. The alien flattened itself against me, shuddering.

And then it began to squeal. *"Weeeeeee-weeeeee!"*

The ground under my feet began to shudder like an earthquake. Suddenly there was a blast —

KA ——— BOOOM!

I whirled as a huge, fat tentacle punched right through the hillside.

REEEE-REEEEEEE-REEEEEEE!

32

The huge alien's shrieks seemed to shatter the air. The noise drilled into my brain until I felt blind and deaf. I knew I was screaming but I couldn't hear a thing except —

REEEEE-REEEEEEE-REEEEEEEEEEEEEEEEE!

A black blob the size of a mountain began to roll and bubble through the hole punched in the hillside. Furious tentacles slashed the air so fast they were a blur.

I grabbed Jessie and jumped to the other side of the crate, putting it between us and the boiling alien. But now the crate seemed awfully puny.

Then suddenly the big alien stopped. Its tentacles flopped to the ground. It continued to pulse, giving off a dark angry light but its body stayed half in, half out of the hill.

I took a breath, feeling the smaller blob quiver against me.

"Nick, look at Mom and Dad!" said Jessie. "What's happened to them? What's happened to all of them?"

I was afraid to take my eyes off the smoldering alien but I threw a quick glance behind me. My heart lurched. I felt like I was looking at an army of statues. Everyone seemed turned to stone.

"Wow, that was close," said Frasier, rubbing his arms as he joined us. "One minute my parents were dragging me off and the next second they just let go. Like that alien pressed their 'off' switch."

Jessie nodded. "I think it was because of that one," she said, indicating our hostage. "The humans didn't care about it. They had their orders — to get us with the other kids — and they didn't see anything else."

"It's like the aliens don't really communicate with the adults," I said wonderingly. "They can make them do things but they can't understand anything."

"Yeah," said Frasier eagerly. "Like a dog does tricks but he doesn't have the vaguest why you want him to."

We fell silent, looking at our parents. They stood, slack-jawed and completely still, except for the constant slithering of their eyes. It made me angry to think of them being treated like dogs or windup toys.

I scowled at the big alien slumped half out of the hill. We'd show them!

Then I noticed something about the huge alien didn't look right. Its tentacles were limp and its pulsing was rapid but dim. "Hey, guys, look," I said. "Does that thing look sick to you?"

"Wouldn't that be nice," Jessie commented.

"Yeah!" exclaimed Frasier. "The tips of its tentacles are

shriveling." He stared at it for a minute. "You know what?" he said wonderingly. "I think the aliens are allergic to our sun! Look at those tentacles. They look burnt. That's why all the tunnels! They can't take the sun!"

"Great," said Jessie sarcastically. "So all we have to do is take off the top of Harley Hill and let the sun pour in and the aliens will fall all over themselves getting off our planet. Terrific plan."

Just then I felt my own personal alien come unstuck from my shoulder. A pang of alarm went through me when I looked down at it. It was pale and milky-looking. It had stopped making its squealing noises.

Before I could think what to do, it slipped off my shirt and began to slide to the ground. I actually had to catch it in my bare hands.

My stomach rose into my throat as glop engulfed my fingers, hands, wrists, arms. Struggling not to puke from disgust, I swallowed hard and gulped for breath.

Resisting the urge to snatch my hands free of the gummy ooze took all my willpower. I hardly had breath left to speak.

"Frasier, quick!" I panted. "Give me your backpack."

"My backpack!" He looked at the creature with dismay. "My backpack?"

"Yes!" I insisted. "I'll put the alien on top of it and we'll slide it into the crate to keep it out of the sun."

Reluctantly, Frasier eased out of his backpack, making faces and moaning as he emptied it.

"Hurry!" I demanded in a strangled voice. My fingers felt so icky I couldn't stand it.

Jessie snatched the backpack from Frasier and dropped it on the ground. As I bent down the creature made a faint noise and feebly tried to crawl up my arm.

But it was too weak. I rolled it onto the backpack where it lay like a puddle of slime-covered dough. Grimacing, Jessie helped me slide the whole thing into the crate.

The alien in the hillside flopped its tentacles when it saw what we were doing but it stayed where it was.

"How are we going to lift the crate?" Jessie asked, looking nervously at the mountainous alien. "The back end is broken."

"No sweat," said Frasier, holding up a roll of duct tape. "It was in my backpack. Duct tape is very useful. You never know when it's going to come in handy."

Once he got the crate taped up we tried lifting it. That got the big alien all worked up again but it still didn't come after us.

"Now let's get out of here," I said nervously. "We'll find someplace safer and decide what to do next."

"But what about that?" asked Jessie, gesturing over her shoulder at the bubbling alien.

"Who cares?" scoffed Frasier. "It can't chase us. We can do what we want."

Famous last words.

As we started off with the crate the big alien began to shriek again.

REEEE-REEEEEEEEE-REEEEEEEEE!

And then another piece of the hillside exploded out-wards.

KA-BOOOOM!

I threw up my arm to ward off the sudden rain of fly-ing dirt and sharp rock shards.

"Ow!" yelled Frasier. "Let's get out of here!"

Awkwardly we began to run with the crate. The alien's shrieks reached such a pitch I felt my head would explode. The terrible sound seemed to paralyze my muscles. Vibrations ran up and down my backbone like shivers of pain.

I glanced back and froze in horror.

The alien was once again boiling out of the hillside. It was even bigger than we'd thought before.

It swelled and bubbled, a massive tidal wave of dark ooze bearing relentlessly down on us.

"Run!" screamed Jessie, snatching up her end of the crate and dragging me and Frasier after her.

But we couldn't possibly escape it. It kept coming, an endless angry stream of goo rolling after us like boiling tar.

Frasier stumbled on the uneven ground. As I pushed him to his feet, I threw a glance backward.

"AAAIII —!"

But what I saw was so horrible it snatched the scream right out of my throat.

33

REEEEE-EEEEEEEE-EEEEEEEE!

The alien had thrown out a tentacle and it was whipping after us. But it was a tentacle unlike any I'd seen before.

The tentacle was thick and covered with a thick layer of green slime. But that wasn't the worst.

The worst was the gaping mouths that popped out all over it. They looked like fleshy suction cups and they gummed the air hungrily as the tentacle homed in on us.

It was like the mouths already imagined how it would feel when they fastened their rubbery lips on us. And they could hardly wait.

"Leave the crate," yelled Jessie. "It's the crate they want, Nick! Leave it and run!"

But I couldn't leave the crate. "No!" I shouted over the piercing noise of the alien's shrieking. "It's all we have. We can't save anybody without it."

"We can't save anybody if we're not around either,"

Frasier shouted in my ear as he pried my hand off the crate. "Come on, Nick. They can't open it anyway. Wood, remember?"

I felt the whoosh of air as Frasier dragged me out from under the desperate grasp of the tentacle. He had forgotten all about his wrenched knee.

But we'd only sprinted a few panicky steps when we heard a thud behind us. And the alien's shrieks grew even more high-pitched.

Risking a glance back, I skidded to a halt, staring in amazement.

The horrible gruesome tentacle now lay flat and limp on the ground, inches from the crate. Its hideous mouths were puckered and still.

"Oh, wow," moaned Jessie. "I think I'm going to be sick."

At the other end of the tentacle, the mountainous alien was writhing. Where the sun hit it, its bubbly goo was starting to blacken, blister, and pop. Dark liquid spurted from it.

Slowly, the alien cringed back into the hillside, pulling the useless tentacle behind it and shrieking horribly.

REEEEEEEEEE-REEEEEEEEEEEEEEEEE!

"Help me with the crate," I said when the huge alien had squeezed most of itself into the hill.

We moved cautiously but the alien did nothing. It even stopped shrieking.

Jessie scowled at it. She pushed her tangled hair behind her ears with a defiant gesture. "Putting the blob in the crate was a good idea, Nick," she said. "As long as it's inside the wooden crate, its friends can't save it, even if they are fifty times bigger than us and can sprout tentacles whenever they want. We're the only ones who can save their friend. Now they need us."

She smiled at the blob in the hillside. It wasn't a pleasant smile.

Frasier nodded with satisfaction. "I knew it," he said. "There's nothing it can do."

I winced, hearing those words. The last time Frasier sounded so confident we nearly got drowned in a tidal wave of alien blubber.

I bent down and looked through the slat at our captive and was relieved to see it was pulsing more brightly again. We picked up the crate and started off.

The big alien twitched and several boulders tumbled down out of the hill. My heart leaped but that was it for the alien. It really did seem defeated this time.

"Where are we going?" asked Jessie.

"We need to find our way back to that cavern where they're keeping the other kids," I said.

"I don't want to go in any more alien tunnels," said Frasier. "Not any sooner than we have to anyway. Let's go back to your house. We can take the old mining tunnel that leads out from your basement. We already know that leads back to the alien spaceship. And I plotted a course with my compass. I can get us to the kids, no sweat."

That old mining tunnel was old and rickety and ready to cave in. But it seemed like home compared to the alien tunnels.

It was a good plan.

As we turned down the hill, thunder rolled ominously. We looked at each other, startled. The sky was sunny and blue, not a cloud in sight.

Thunder sounded again, louder. We looked up, over Harley Hill. And our hearts sank right into despair.

Over the top of the hill a glowing cloud was forming. Its dark underside boiled angrily, expanding every second.

Lightning flashed and crackled inside it. Bolts struck one another like huge swords clanging together before a fight.

The aliens weren't done with us yet.

34

The cloud gathered force, expanding so rapidly its menacing shadow overtook us and raced ahead down the hill.

In minutes the sun was blotted out over our heads although we could still see it shining brightly to the east where the town would be. The hillside turned dark and the temperature plunged.

Although we'd been sweating a second ago, we were now shivering and not just with fear. It was freezing. My fingers felt numb where they clutched the crate.

We quickened our pace but we knew it was useless. We were as powerless as ants under the widening alien cloud.

"This m-must be how the aliens g-get around their problem with the s-sun," Jessie said through chattering teeth.

But when we looked to see if the big alien was after us again, it hadn't moved. Did that mean it was too hurt and it was going to leave our fate to other, fresher aliens?

I shuddered, feeling queasy with panic. My eyes darted everywhere looking for lurking alien hulks and whip-fast tentacles.

Overhead the seething cloud foamed and churned, casting its eerie glow over us. Lightning flashed angrily, arcing from one side of the cloud to the other and back again.

"I think we should leave the crate," said Frasier, his eyes wide with terror. "If we leave the crate maybe they'll let us go."

Scared as I was, determination clamped around my heart like a vise.

"No." I bit down hard to try and keep my teeth from chattering. "They've taken over our parents and seized a whole school full of kids. All we've done is take one small blob and they act like it's the end of the world. I'm not leaving the crate."

"It doesn't matter anyway, Frasier," said Jessie, hunching her shoulders as she jumped at shadows, imagining tentacles. "They can't open the crate themselves, remember? They need at least one of us. They're not going to let us off this hill."

As if to prove her wrong about needing us and right about not letting us off the hill, the cloud above suddenly opened up.

CRRR-AAAACK!

A jagged bolt of lightning struck the earth inches in

front of my toes. My hand ripped off the crate and I was lifted ten feet into the sky.

For an instant I seemed to float head over heels, surrounded by strange sparkles. I was deafened from the blast of thunder and my mind was blanked out by the flash.

Then I slammed back to earth flat on my back. All around me, gold-sparkled rocks rained onto the ground, making starlike patterns in the weird alien glow.

When one thumped me on the chest, I came to my senses.

"Nick! Get up, we've got to get out of here!" Jessie was shouting as Frasier tugged on my arm.

Her hair was whipping around her face in the sudden wind. Lightning flashes from inside the cloud lit up the fear on her face.

I jumped to my feet, anger pumping through my heart as fiercely as fear. "Grab the crate," I said.

"What, are you crazy?" Frasier shouted over the crash of thunder, his eyes wild.

"Haul it up!" I demanded. "We'll hold it over our heads. They won't dare blast their precious blob!"

Quickly the three of us hauled the crate high enough to crawl under. The storm built to a frenzy. We could barely keep our grip on the edge of the crate.

"What now?" yelled Jessie.

"Head downhill," I yelled back.

A bolt of lightning struck at Frasier's feet. They went

out from under him and the crate fell on his chest. His bat went flying and instantly a bolt of lightning struck it. The bat was in flames before it hit the ground.

Hurriedly, we helped Frasier up, keeping as much of ourselves as we could under the crate.

Again we struggled to our feet and pointed ourselves downhill. We'd only taken one step when two bolts of lightning struck simultaneously, gouging the ground under my feet and Jessie's feet.

We jumped backward as sparkly rocks blasted into the air. Another bolt quickly followed, chasing us back against the hill.

Thunder crashed so loud we couldn't speak. Whenever we stopped, lightning struck behind us and we jumped forward again.

The lightning was forcing us along the side of the hill. My nerves jangled as heat seared my toes. The deafening crack of the lightning clashed with the boom of thunder, scrambling my wits.

We couldn't think, couldn't hear, couldn't speak. All we could do was keep moving, dancing inches in front of the lightning.

Suddenly Jessie pounded my arm and pointed frantically. I looked. There against the hill was what looked like a cave.

Safety! Hope clutched at my heart. My stomach constricted. We eyed each other and all at once broke into a run, keeping step so we didn't drop the crate, our only shield.

The lightning seemed to double in intensity, striking sparks off our heels. More rocks blasted up from the ground, pelting us with sparkles.

I kept my eyes on the cave opening, hoping it was deep enough for us to escape the lightning.

Wind buffeted us sideways and I stumbled. I threw out my arm to keep myself from hitting the ground. A bolt of lightning struck like a knife between two of my fingers.

I leaped to my feet and my heart took off like a machine gun.

We were almost there. The cave yawned dark and welcoming. I hardly dared to think we'd really make it and then all of a sudden we were inside!

Lightning struck furiously all across the entrance. But it was powerless to reach us.

We set down the crate and sprawled on the ground, struggling to catch our breath.

After a while my heart settled into a terrified pounding I now thought of as normal. I sat up and looked around.

Lightning flashed so I got a good look.

"Wow," groaned Jessie, staring at the back of the cave with dread. "Out of the fire and into *real* trouble."

35

Outside the cave, the turbulent wind had died down. The eerie glow had faded but an occasional lightning bolt still struck in front of the entrance as if to remind us we wouldn't be going anywhere.

"They've got us right where they want us," complained Frasier.

The wide opening of the cave narrowed into a tunnel which burrowed into the hillside, back toward the mothership. In the lightning flashes we could make out the smooth swirls of alien melted rock.

We fell silent, too exhausted to figure out what to do next. After a few minutes I got up and peeked into the crate. The little alien blob was bubbling again and seemed to be pulsing normally. It gave off a rosy light.

Frasier scowled at me. "Before, when my zombie parents snatched me," he said, "you said you were going to mash that blob into the wood but you didn't. How come?" he asked accusingly.

Jessie sighed. "It wouldn't have done any good, Frasier. We agreed on that."

"Yes, but Nick didn't know that at that moment, did you?"

I shrugged uncomfortably. "I couldn't," I told him. "I think it's a little one."

"That's pretty obvious," said Frasier. "Since the other ones are big enough to bulldoze mountains."

"I mean little, like a child," I said. "Alien junior."

They both looked at me openmouthed. "Just because it's small —" Jessie began.

I interrupted her. "It *communicated* with me," I said. "By pictures. But the proportions were wrong. The pictures reminded me of something a first-grader might do. Plus it seemed curious. And kind of friendly. Like it trusted me."

Frasier sat up, instantly alert. "Pictures? So that's how you know there's something wrong with the spaceship?"

"Right. First it showed the spaceship gliding through space," I explained. "Then it focused in on the back end and showed puffs of smoke coming out — as if a spaceship would puff smoke, right? Then it showed the puffs stopping and the ship falling out of the sky and crashing into earth."

Frasier looked thoughtful. "Let's eat," he said. "And think about this."

He pulled an MRE out of his pocket. Jessie and I did the same. They were pretty mangled and squished but my mouth began to water anyway. I couldn't remember the last time I'd eaten.

I stuck a mouthful of something that looked like dried hairball into my mouth. It tasted like wet fur.

We chewed in silence for a while. Then Jessie got to her knees and peered into the crate. I scooted beside her. The blob bubbled and sprouted a small tentacle.

It kind of waved at us and angled toward the slat opening. But an inch away it recoiled and the whole tentacle snapped back inside the blob. The blob pulsed faster, like it was agitated.

"Did it stick one of those tentacles in your ear to communicate?" asked Jessie.

"Not really," I said evasively. "I don't particularly want to talk about it."

Frasier snapped his fingers. "The ship ran out of fuel!" he exclaimed. "That has to be it. Otherwise the creature would have shown the engines, not puffs of smoke."

"Maybe it doesn't know what the engines look like," said Jessie.

Frasier shook his head. "The big ones must have been running — or tentacling — around frantically and gabbling about what was wrong. If it was the engines they would have been working on them and that's what your blob would have shown." He looked pleased with himself.

"I thought the same thing," I told him. "But how does it help? We don't know what they use for fuel. Or even if earth has any of whatever it is."

"Maybe they use human brains for fuel," said Jessie. "And all they need is a few more."

Before any of us could think of a reason why that probably wasn't true, a bolt of lightning struck the hillside over our cave. The jagged bolt punched a hole in the ceiling and chunks of rock rained down.

We scrambled to our feet, dropping the remains of our MREs.

"I think they've decided we had enough rest," I said.

We looked into the darkness of the alien tunnel. I'd lost my flashlight somewhere but Jessie and Frasier still had theirs. They clicked them on.

Frasier checked his compass and consulted a scrap of paper from his pocket. "I think I can get us to the kids from here," he said.

Then he looked at the crate. "It's a real drag lugging that thing around," he said, looking at me speculatively. "Couldn't you —?"

I shuddered. "No way. Besides it might escape. I think it only glommed on to me before because the communicating exhausted it."

"And we need the wood," said Jessie, gripping one end of the crate. "It's our only defense."

We started into the tunnel, feeling its silence like a weight.

36

"This is creepy," said Jessie. "I feel as if we're being watched."

We kept looking over our shoulders and shining the flashlights into shadows on the walls. But nothing leaped out at us. Nothing moved.

But we couldn't shake the feeling of unfriendly eyes boring into our backs.

Suddenly a large dark shape loomed out of the wall. With a frightened shout, Frasier and Jessie both whipped their flashlight beams at it.

The flashlight beams kept going, swallowed up by the black shape. I gasped in horror but Jessie let go of the crate and started forward, right at the thing! A second later, she disappeared.

"Jessie!" I cried.

Then her voice bounced back to us. "It's another tunnel," she called. "Which way should we go?"

The air seemed to stir as if agitated. "Come back,

Jessie," I called out, flutters stirring in my stomach. "We've got to stay together. Near the crate."

"Oops, you're right," she said. Her running footsteps echoed loudly in the empty tunnel. I held my breath until she was back with us.

Frasier consulted his compass and his scrap of paper again. "The cavern with our friends is this way," he said, pointing into the new tunnel. "It shouldn't be far."

We picked up the crate and started into the new tunnel. It was narrower and seemed even darker than the other one. But I pushed aside my uneasiness by thinking about our friends. I even imagined I was hearing their voices.

"Listen," said Jessie, with a catch of excitement. "Is that —"

REEEEE-REEEEEEEE-REEEEEEEE!

We fell to our knees, clapping our hands over our ears. The flashlights fell to the ground and rolled.

The alien noise racketed off the walls, bombarding us. It was so piercing I cringed, expecting the walls to shatter and bury us. Suddenly the air compressed, squeezing us as if a train was hurtling through the tunnel right at us.

Jessie snatched up her flashlight and pointed it down the tunnel. She screamed, although the sound was immediately swallowed by the increasing alien shrieks.

REEEEEEEEEE-REEEEEEE-REEEEEEEEEEEEE!

Jessie jumped to her feet and tugged at my arm. She

was mouthing something but I couldn't hear what it was. The air rushed past me, thick and turbulent. My head was spinning. Again Jessie pointed urgently with her flashlight.

I felt my heart stop. A bulging black cloud was rushing toward us, and then I saw the tentacles erupting from it. They slashed the air as they stretched toward us like strings of drool with muscles.

Frasier was still hunched over on the floor with his arms covering his head. Jessie and I grabbed him and pointed. Somehow we remembered to snatch up the crate as we fled back the way we'd come.

We reached the junction of the two tunnels and automatically turned toward the cave. But we'd only taken a step or two when the shrieks got louder.

REEEEE-REEEEEEEEE-REEEEEE!

Now they were coming from two directions. In the dimming flashlight beams we saw another dark blob bearing down on us from the cave end of the tunnel.

We had no choice. We had to go deeper into the hill. Reversing direction we ran again, wondering if the two blobs would come together at the tunnel junction, squishing us between them.

My head thumped with noise and fear. As we approached the other tunnel opening, Frasier's light beam caught on a tentacle snaking across the floor. There was no time to stop.

Without thinking, all three of us soared into the air.

We came down running. Somehow the tentacle had missed us.

Then the tunnel in front of us began to glow. My heart crashed. It was obvious the aliens had a plan and we were racing full tilt right into it. But what choice did we have?

I glanced back over my shoulder just in time to see the blobs from the two tunnels collide. A puff of gas belched up between them. Then they melted together, bubbling over at the seams, goo spattering the walls.

My feet felt a little lighter as I realized we were gaining on them as they reeled from the impact. But when I glanced back a second later, the blob was rolling after us again.

Only this time it was twice as big and had twice as many tentacles, with more sprouting and pushing it along every instant.

A sudden noise snapped my head back around.

CRRR — ACK!

Jessie swung her flashlight at the sound. *"AAAH!"* She screamed and dropped the flashlight. It rolled and I heard a tentacle suck it up like candy.

But I didn't need any more light to see the crack in the tunnel wall. Or the black ooze that was pushing out of it.

CR — AACK
CRAAA — CK!

37

My eyes twitched to the right and left but I couldn't move my head fast enough to keep up with the pattern of cracks fissuring the walls around us.

CRR — ACK! CRACK! CRA — CK!

Black goo wriggled, gushed, and streamed out of every crack, trickling down the walls or forming huge bubbles which popped over our heads like bubblegum, spattering us with slime.

Globs of the stuff fell, then sprouted tentacles and pushed up off the tunnel floor to head after us. Terror seemed to give our feet wings. All we could do was keep running.

But none of us lost our grip on the crate. Yippy squealing noises were coming out of it. We could hear them because the blobs had gone silent. They seemed to be saving their energy for chasing us.

I was afraid to look back and afraid not to. Finally I couldn't stand it anymore. I looked and immediately wished I hadn't.

The tunnel was filled floor to ceiling with huge lumpy blobs. More cracks were opening every second, pouring gobs of mucky goo down onto the blob.

Tentacles swarmed ahead of the blobs. Even as I watched, one of the tentacles shot up into the air and stretched, falling almost close enough to nip at our heels.

"Faster," I screeched, my throat feeling like sandpaper.

My lungs were burning and my legs felt rubbery. I knew Frasier and Jessie must be feeling the same. I could hear their harsh breathing whistling through their lungs. But somehow we ran even faster.

How long can this tunnel go on? I wondered in desperation. Even as the thought passed through my mind the tunnel widened. And then all of a sudden we were in a place we knew.

The tunnel opened into a huge space where stone stalactites melted into strange metal formations, like struts in an airplane hangar.

This was the place we'd stumbled onto the first time we explored the alien tunnels. Only it was different now. The struts were straighter, not so crumpled looking. And the metal and stone ran in separate veins, side by side.

I realized the aliens must have repaired the damage the crash had done.

I glanced back. The blobs were closer. Tentacles writhed in excitement and the black blobs bumped and rolled over one another in their eagerness to get us.

We had to keep going. But from here there was only one place to go.

Sick fear stirred in my stomach as we approached the sheer wall at the end of the stalacite-strut area.

I knew from before that there was a small opening at the bottom of the wall. And behind the wall was nothing but a bubbling pool of thick, syrupy, glowing liquid filled with things we couldn't see.

We were going so fast we ran into the wall before we could stop ourselves.

Frasier dropped to the floor and began scrambling through the narrow opening in the wall.

"Wait!" rasped Jessie, grabbing his shirt.

Frasier shot a wild-eyed look over his shoulder. "They're coming," he gasped hoarsely. "We have to."

The aliens were boiling over one another, gushing along the floor, spitting out tentacles. In another minute they'd catch us.

The sight filled me with such horror all my insides seemed to stick together in a knotted mass. I dropped to the floor. "Quick, go!" I urged. "I'll push the crate in to you. Put it between you and the pool."

A ripple of fear washed over Jessie's face. She dove after Frasier. I heard a tentacle slap behind me. In my hurry, I got the crate jammed in the narrow opening.

It wouldn't move. I could hear the slurping, sucking sounds the blobs made rushing across the floor. Jessie and Frasier wiggled the crate desperately but it didn't budge. I moaned.

A slithering noise drilled into my brain. I shoved at the crate.

Then I felt the slimy cold touch of a tentacle snapping around my ankle.

38

"YAAAAAAAAAAA!" I shrieked. Icy terror surged into my muscles. I rammed my shoulder against the crate and it yielded with a splintering sound.

The tentacle tightened around my ankle. I hurled myself through the opening, feeling my leg stretch like a rubber band. I kicked out, slamming the slimy tentacle against the rock wall.

It let go with a squishy sucking sound and I fell through the opening. I slid, unable to stop myself. The pool was there, rippling quietly.

I was headed straight for it.

With horror I felt myself go over the edge. My fingers scrabbled for a hold but the rock ledge was too wet and smooth.

Frasier shouted and hands grabbed me. I gasped like a fish, my nose an inch from the scummy surface. Frasier and Jessie hauled me back onto the ledge overlooking the pool. I was shaking so hard they had trouble holding on to me.

The ledge was just wide enough for us to scrunch against the wall with the crate in front of us, between us and the pool. The little blob inside began to make its little noises again.

"*Weeeee-weeeee.*"

The surface of the pool began to agitate ominously. The gentle ripples became waves and slapped against the rock sides of the pool.

Shapes began to stir in the glowing depths.

I stared at the pool, my stomach sloshing. "I don't think we have much time," I said, feeling my mouth go dry. "We have to find out what the mothership uses for fuel. It's our only chance."

"Sure," said Jessie, scraping hair out of her eyes. "But how are we going to find out?"

"There's only one way," I said, shuddering. "I just wish I was sure it would work. I'll have to communicate with the alien baby again."

Jessie sucked in her breath.

"How?" asked Frasier.

A wave of revulsion swept over me as I pictured it. I slid around toward the narrow end of the crate and slid open the panel. "I have to let it ooze over my head," I said.

There was a shocked silence. I lay down on the ledge and began to slide my head into the crate. At the first clammy touch of the alien, shudders spasmed through me. My stomach heaved up in my throat.

I swallowed, hard. Then suddenly I was engulfed in

warmth. I was sinking into ooze. It covered me like the softest, warmest blanket. It lapped over my eyes, welled up into my nose and spilled down my throat, filling my stomach like sweet pudding.

My muscles relaxed as I sank deeper, deeper. I felt wonderful. I couldn't imagine any reason to ever surface again.

39

My mind blinked. Panic charged through me, jerking my arms and legs. I was smothering! Drowning!

The alien was taking me over!

I kicked and choked. I was a boy, not a blob!

Suddenly a sound came into my head. *Xxslypzx.* The clinging goo receded from my face and I took in huge gulps of spicy-smelling air. I was a boy, not a *xxslypzx*.

I found myself floating on top of the ooze. It was as soft and pleasant as a feather pillow. I tried out the sound in my head, *xxslypzx*. Where are you, *xxslypzx*?

Deep inside, somewhere beyond the boundaries of me, I heard another sound. *"Weeeee-weeeeee."* I saw a picture of the pool and an aching, longing, yearning feeling came over me. But this time I could tell it wasn't my feeling. It was the alien.

Experiencing its confusion and sadness, I felt awful for kidnapping it. "Soon," I projected soothingly. "Soon." Then I showed it a picture of all our school friends trapped like cattle in the alien cavern and our parents moving like puppets. "We have to free them," I told it.

Uncertain feelings stirred within me. It didn't really understand. It just wanted to get back into that pool.

Suddenly I felt a tug on my foot, than another, more urgent. The tug was coming from outside. Frasier or Jessie was trying to warn me of something. But I couldn't break off communication now. We'd hardly started.

Quickly, I formed a picture in my mind of the alien spaceship taking off from Earth in a huge blast of smoke. A wave of joy from the alien burst through me.

"How do we help?" I asked. "What does your ship use for fuel?" Carefully, I pictured the exhaust end of the ship, the rich smoke streaming out of it.

Without warning a jagged bolt of lightning sliced through my brain. *CRACK!* It struck the ground sending up a huge shower of sparkly rocks.

A picture of the ship formed. Tentacled aliens funneled the rocks inside. The ship blasted off.

The rocks!?

But before I could let it know I understood, and explain how everyone would have to be freed before we would help, something jerked me. I felt the connection rip. The alien congealed in sudden terror and huddled in a corner of my mind.

There was another hard pull. As the alien began to disappear, I quickly sent it a soothing vision of slipping into the pool.

Then I was blinking on the stone ledge and Frasier

and Jessie were trying to shove me behind the crate. They were both bug-eyed with fear.

There was a strange furious hissing noise all around us.

Frasier had a slat from the crate in his hand and was beating the air behind him while Jessie shook me.

"Nick, are you awake?" Jessie demanded urgently. "We're surrounded. They're never going to let us out. They got really mad as soon as you put your head in the crate. They're in a frenzy!"

As she spoke, I realized the pool chamber was thick with tentacles, like a can full of bait worms.

Some came up out of the surface of the pool but most of them were crowding through the small opening in the wall. They hissed angrily, spitting out gobs of slime.

Outside the chamber I heard heavy sloshing sounds, like tons and tons of blubber pushing and shoving through a crowd. Tentacles slapped the walls outside, making a wet smacking noise that started a quivering action in my stomach.

The ledge was thick with fat writhing tentacles. The only clear space was right around the wooden crate.

"I think the whole shipful of them is pressing in on this chamber," said Frasier, his eyes darting. "I feel like the walls are giving way. This is the maddest they've ever been. I don't see how we're going to get out of this one."

Jessie cried out and pounced on my head.

WHAP!

40

A tentacle as thick as a fire hose whipped against the wall where my head had been.

"We've got to keep our heads down," Jessie said in what I thought was the understatement of the day.

Tentacles whizzed furiously over our heads and slapped down on the ledge, inches from the crate.

Inside the crate the little blob made its scared, squealing baby noises.

I couldn't stand listening to it. Now that I knew how the poor *xxslypzx* felt, my stomach rolled at every bleat. It was just a baby. It wasn't its fault that all the adult aliens were horrible creeps and invaders.

Before Jessie and Frasier could stop me, I tipped the crate up and let the little alien slide into the pool.

Xxslypzx was free, back with his own kind.

The sudden stillness in the chamber felt like a shock wave. Every tentacle froze in place. Every noise stopped. The only sound was the soft lapping of the pool.

"What have you done?" breathed Jessie.

"Now we really have lost our last hope," moaned Frasier.

"I know what they use for fuel," I said. "But I don't know how we're going to tell them we know. You pulled me away just as the alien was showing me the fuel."

"Well? What is it?" asked Frasier.

"Those sparkly rocks the lightning was kicking up," I answered. "But they'll never let us out of here to get them some."

"Mica?!" shouted Frasier, causing several tentacles to twitch in our direction again. "They use mica?" Forgetting the aliens in his excitement, Frasier dropped the wooden slat and slid sideways to fumble in his pockets.

Jessie and I lunged for him but the alien was quicker. Hissing, the tentacle grabbed his arm and yanked Frasier backward. A bright gold, sparkling pebble flew out of his hand. It rolled across the stone ledge and dropped with a gentle plop into the pool.

The tentacle let go instantly. All other tentacles in the chamber snapped to attention. Their quivering tips turned like periscopes to face us.

"I picked some up," said Frasier, grinning. "For my rock collection. Of course, mica is no big deal but when it's blasted out of the ground by alien lightning then I figure I should keep some." He opened his fist, showing two more chunks.

"SSSSSSSsssssss!"

The tentacles hissed in unison. Several darted forward over Frasier's head. He closed his fist over the rocks and they retreated. Cautiously he stepped out from behind the crate, holding the rocks up. The tentacles receded away from him.

"I think we can leave," said Frasier. "I think they get the idea."

"Let's take the crate anyway," said Jessie. "We can always crawl into it if it turns out you're wrong."

"I don't know how you think we're going to get past that," I said, gesturing at the room's only entrance.

The small opening was squashed full of tentacles. Frasier stepped confidently forward, waving his rocks. He wasn't even holding an end of the crate. He made shooing motions.

For a second the tentacles stuck in the entrance as all of them tried to get out at once. Then the way was clear.

We exchanged glances of wonder, then quickly squeezed through. Outside the chamber, things were different. My heart lurched against my ribs.

Huge lumpy blobs squatted outside the chamber, waving their tentacles with lazy menace. We couldn't see their eyes but we knew they were staring at us distrustfully.

Frasier took one of his precious mica rocks and bowled it down the floor ahead of us. Tentacles snapped toward it but none picked it up. They just batted it along ahead of us.

I began to feel like we were going to get out of this.

We entered the big airplane hangar room and my heart began to pound again.

The walls were lined with blobs. It looked like the whole huge chamber was made of pulsing, boiling, unpredictable blubber. Blobs hung from the struts by tentacles, dripping goo onto blobs below.

I jumped as a tentacle slashed out at my feet and another lashed over my head. But both retreated without touching us.

We walked through, toward the tunnel. And there my heart sank. There was no more tunnel. Just a tube packed full of goo.

But as we stared at it in dismay, the black blobs began to ooze back into the cracks in the tunnel walls. This continued until there was a narrow space free. It was large enough to walk through single file, if we kept our arms clasped against our sides.

We waited but the aliens were done moving. "Let's go," said Jessie impatiently. "If I don't get some air soon I'm going to scream."

"Easy for you to say," Frasier argued. "You're the skinniest. I'll never make it through there without touching one."

Then, with a noise of disgust, Frasier started into the tunnel. I kept my breathing shallow. The crate helped. The aliens recoiled from it, hissing. But still, I had to swallow my stomach every few minutes.

The tunnel went on forever. I began to feel like it would never end.

And then, at last, daylight.

We didn't waste any time. We scurried around gathering mica as fast as we could, mostly from around the lightning strikes where it was already blasted out of the ground.

When we had the crate full, we hauled it back to the cave opening. Tentacles yearned toward it. Dozens of them wound over each other with excitement.

But, of course, they couldn't get at the crate. "We'll empty it when you free our friends and parents," I announced. We acted it out, pantomiming like crazy but of course we couldn't tell whether they got it or not.

The blobs acted more agitated, throwing out huge bubbles which burst in clouds of steam. Tentacles erupted from their bodies only to be sucked back in again.

Then we felt a deep rumble under our feet. The ground began to shake. Cold slithered up my backbone. It felt like an earthquake. A big one.

Then we heard an explosion, like a volcano erupting deep underground. The awful sound reverberated in my heart like a steel drum.

"What's that?" cried Frasier.

Suddenly we heard crying and screaming. Our friends!

41

Without thinking we ripped off pieces of the crate and raced back into the tunnel.

Frasier waved his wooden slat like a sword as we ran through the tunnel. On either side, blobs cringed away.

Where the blobs touched each other they boiled furiously, sending up geysers of goo. They were making a strange angry noise, like pots of boiling glue foaming over on a hot stove.

"Heeelp! Heeeelp us!"

I felt furious. Here we had freed our only captive, gathered fuel for these creeps, and they were still attacking! "At least they'll never get that crate open without us," I said through clenched teeth.

"What makes you say that?" asked Jessie, hair flying out behind her. "All they have to do is get our parents to empty the crate. Simple. They don't need us anymore."

As if to show how true that was, a tentacle whipped out and snapped itself around Frasier's waist, sweeping him off his feet. Frasier shouted and pulled back his hand to smack the thing with his wooden weapon.

But another tentacle snapped out of the opposite side of the tunnel and seized his wrist. We saw the wrist bend into an impossible angle.

Frasier screamed and dropped the slat.

The tentacles whipped him away, passing him down the line of aliens like a party toy.

As Jessie and I began to lash out angrily at all the blobs around us, more tentacles swooped down and coiled around us. I heard Jessie cry out just as a second tentacle forced me to drop my wood.

Then it tossed me to the next blob which hissed loudly as it grabbed me by the legs and swung me on.

"HELP! GET US OUT OF HERE!"

I could hear our school friends' voices, loud and clear now. The aliens were going to dump us in with them. Did they plan to take us back to their planet?

Or just leave us trapped inside the hill forever?

The air shuddered. I flew head over heels. As the next alien caught me, it shook as if the ground had shifted under its feet.

BOOOOM!

42

The blast was deafening.

The sound of kids' voices got very loud. They were screaming and laughing and crying.

Then suddenly I was sprawled on the smooth surface of the tunnel floor. There were no tentacles around. But Frasier and Jessie were there.

We wobbled to our feet, feeling dazed.

The smell of molten rock drifted to us a second before the rock wall in front of us parted with a sizzling *CRACK!* and melted in two separate streams.

On the other side of the wall was the cavern with the kids in it! We dashed through the opening.

"HELP! GET US OUT!" they yelled.

Part of the cavern wall had caved in. Kids were climbing up, scrambling over the fallen rocks.

But as we ran forward to help, the ground shifted under our feet again.

BOOOOOM!

Another section of the cavern wall caved in, half melting, half exploding. Somehow it didn't hit any kids.

Then the ground began shaking harder and harder. We hauled our friends up out of the cavern as fast as we could. A tremendous rumbling noise built somewhere under our feet.

It felt like all of Harley Hill was about to go up like a volcano.

"It sounds like an engine starting," Frasier shouted. "A really *huge* engine!"

We hurried the last of the little kids out of the cavern. "Hurry!" we yelled. "Follow us!"

We led the way back into the tunnel. The blobs were gone. All of them. There was nothing but smooth, shiny rock. Not even a smear of ooze anywhere.

When we reached the cave, Mom and Dad, and Frasier's parents, too, were milling around in a daze. The crate had been upended and emptied — no surprise.

"There you are," cried Mom, sounding overjoyed. "We've been looking everywhere for you kids!"

She ran forward and grabbed both me and Jessie in a hug, Dad right behind her. Frasier's parents were all over him, too, scolding and relieved.

They were really themselves again!

Outside we heard shouts of greeting and joy as parents and kids found each other.

"What were you doing out here this time of night?" asked Dad. He frowned like he was trying to think of something that might be important.

"You'd never believe us," Jessie said, grinning at me.

"Try me," said Mom.

"Well, first this alien spaceship crashed into the hills. Then these slimy tentacles —"

"You're right," said Dad. "We don't believe you."

But just then the cave floor began to buckle under us. We ran outside but the whole hill was shaking like it was coming apart.

The top of Harley Hill began to glow red-hot. It glowed hotter and hotter until in a huge puff of steam the rock evaporated, leaving a crater!

As we stared, the sleek silvery form of the giant alien mothership lifted out of the crater — so huge it blocked the stars from the sky. It hovered in a blaze of light, blinding us, until finally it zoomed off into the dark sky, going higher and higher, leaving earth behind as it headed into outer space.

We watched until even the faint trail of light it made had disappeared. The whole crowd was stunned into silence.

But finally Dad stirred. "I have a suggestion," he said. "Let's go home and pretend none of this ever happened."

In twos and threes people began to turn away and drift back to town, their children clutched close beside them.

Jessie leaned over toward me and Frasier. "Do you think they'll ever come back?" she whispered.

"I hope so," Frasier said wistfully, his eyes still in the sky.

I stared at him and shook my head. "Frasier, you know what? You *are* an alien!"